Barbara Else works as a freelance writer and editor. Her short stories have been published in a variety of magazines and broadcast on radio. She has also written plays for children and adults. This is her first published novel.

With her husband Chris Else, Barbara runs Total Fiction Services, a manuscript assessment service and literary agency. She has been active in the New Zealand Society of Authors (PEN Inc.) for a number of years.

Barbara lives in the Wellington suburb of Ngaio. Her favourite activities, apart from writing, are gardening, reading and conversing over a bottle of good wine with anyone who will encourage her.

with best wishes

Barbara Else.

THE WARRIOR QUEEN

Barbara Else

GODWIT

To Chris,
for his astonishing persistence

Part of chapter one was first published in *Metro* magazine

Published by Godwit Publishing Ltd
P.O. Box 34-683, Birkenhead
Auckland, New Zealand

First published 1995
6th reprint 1998

ISBN 0 908877 61 7

The publishers acknowledge the assistance of
the Literature Programme of the Arts Council of New Zealand
Toi Aotearoa

Cover design: Christine Hansen
Cover illustration: Megan Jenkinson
Typeset by Orca Publishing Services Ltd, Christchurch
Printed in Hong Kong

Oh! Oh! Oh! Gloomy news!
— Euripides

1
Hot Chips

[ANTICIPATION]

chapter one

Kate's in bed in a hotel, looking at her homework. She's forty-one years old, doing homework on holiday. The words on the paper are in Cyrillic script and there's a picture of a coin. It must be a Russian coin, she thinks. Kate no longer knows why it's important for her to do homework at her age but she supposes she had a good reason when she decided to take Russian.

She looks at the paper. The meaning is trapped in the words, the strangely formed letters, and won't come out. The first capital letter looks like a parrot.

Maybe she'd rather go to the Taronga Park Zoo. She might enjoy the boat trip. Zoos are places to visit when you're away from home. But she doesn't want to go there on her own.

Neither of the others will go with her. Jessica says she's too old for zoos: Mum, they're cruel, and I don't think they're Green! Besides, she's made a friend in the hotel and the girls spend time together, going into shops, smiling at gorgeous guys, smothering laughs behind their hands, making sure they're noticed as they deserve to be, elegant and awkward, young, exuberant.

Richard's here too, but not on holiday. Kate doesn't think Richard ever has a holiday as normal people understand the word, though once or twice a year he has time off for scheduled enjoyment. On this trip, Richard's at a conference. He drew up the agenda: it took weeks of faxes back and forth across the Tasman, long evenings in his study while his bald patch got mottled and his remaining hair stood up all fluffy. Each day he says: **Aren't you enjoying yourself? This took a lot of organising on my part. It's not asking much to expect a word of thanks.** And he looks really hurt.

They are three people crushed into a small hotel room because someone's secretary screwed up the travel arrangements. Thank God there's a secretary to take the blame, thinks Kate: it's a big conference and something had to get screwed. It won't be me, in this small room with a teenage daughter sleeping in the fold-out bed which she doesn't fold away during the day. Why should she? It's her space. Kate's glad Jessica has a space to herself.

Haven't I said thank you? she thinks. I'm sure I would have remembered to say thank you somehow or other. Damn, I wish I had remembered. She wishes she could remember if she'd said it or not, or if Richard's just being a pain.

He's gone down to breakfast. He got out of bed and stalked around like a thunder clap with no clothes on. He doesn't stalk around naked at home; he wears pyjamas and holds the pants fiercely closed. Kate knew what he was thinking: **I'm paying for this room, I'll do just what I like for once.**

His bottom, tight and plump as a football, marched into the bathroom. Jessica glanced at Kate. Kate glanced at her too. The looks flicked away. When Richard's around, sometimes the rest of the family stay quiet. Their thoughts are packed away, like suitcases, carefully labelled, in the attic. Though right then Jess lifted a long thin teenage arm and pointed at the top of her own head. She giggled, not looking at her mother. Kate pulled the sheet up so Richard wouldn't hear her laugh too. The Barometer, Jess meant. Richard's bald patch, blotchy red, which means full organising mode so stand back please, dogs and small children at the rear for safety, well back, thank you.

Kate knows she doesn't look grateful she's on holiday. The smog in Sydney this year is making headlines. She's got the worst cold she's had for years and the worst period pains she's ever had. They were the worst last month too. Each month Richard says: **Sorry, I was going to do something about that. I'll speak to Martin. There's a new drug on the market that's supposed to do wonders. I could prescribe it myself but you ought to see Martin first. We should do this properly. But I'll do it for you. If that's what you want.**

If she says please, that would be great, he'll Frown (the Frown that comes with a capital F). He'll say, we really ought to do it properly. If she says no, that's OK, he'll forget to talk to Martin till next month. Kate always says it's OK. It's only a problem for two days. Two out of thirty-odd is fine.

And Kate looks at it this way: because each month he says he was going to do something, it's proof he cares about her. He just gets tied up in his work. And each month, because she doesn't fuss and nag, it's proof she cares about him. It's nice, to still care about each other after more than twenty years. And Richard does think that things should be done properly. She's glad someone in the household does things properly. I'm glad it doesn't have to be me, she thinks.

Richard likes her to have holidays. He likes her to come to conferences. He likes her to dress up and go with him to the functions in the evening. During the day she can shop. He likes to see what she buys: **That must have been cheaper than back home. You're well set up now, aren't you.**

Books are the only things cheaper than back home. Kate has bought a book of short stories by Elizabeth Jolley. She hasn't shown it to Richard, though she isn't sure if Elizabeth Jolley is feminist or just intelligent.

She's bought a red dress covered in wild patches of orange and yellow, edged with satin and with ribbons on the sleeves.

It's a bold, gypsy dress, exotic. It was amazingly expensive but she coveted it and so she bought it. She'll probably wear it, once, maybe twice. She bought a plain black dress which will be useful if she ever has to go to a funeral. She bought a purple silk shirt long enough to wear with nothing underneath if she ever wants to. She nearly bought a scarf.

She has bought presents for the ones she loves back home. A pair of embroidered braces and two CDs for her trendy son Owen. A book on 'Good Ocker Meals Fast' and a bark painting for her brilliant older daughter Alice, as well as a T-shirt and some tights. She has bought a necklace and a red leather bag for her arty sister. The necklace is made of coins – they might be Russian coins – and funny links shaped like the letter Z. She bought a palette of eye make-up for her niece who's just a bit younger than Jessica. She found a pair of earrings, eucalyptus leaves dipped in gold, for her best friend Libby. She has walked up and down the walks in the Queen Victoria Building; the Prince of Wales Walk, the Grand Walk and all the other walks. She bought an almond croissant and a cappuccino and watched the tourists gather for the pageant in the Royal Clock when it struck the hour. Everyone laughed when Charles I had his head cut off. She tried on bathing suits and giggled when they made her look like something in the crazy mirror at a carnival. The shop assistant asked if she was all right.

Kate's been to the shops every day for four days. There are two more days before they go home. The other wives seem to love shopping but Kate thinks she'll scream if she has to go into one more huge department store, one more teeny wee boutique. She could go on a bus trip, but she did them all when they came to a conference here last year.

She looks at her homework again. She likes the Cyrillic parrot. Maybe this paper tells her in Russian how much it costs to buy one. She liked the parrots at the Melbourne Zoo when they were at a conference there three years ago. One of them clambered along the bars and bobbed up and down. She bobbed back. In a broad Australian accent it said, *Do you wanna dreenk? Do you wanna dreenk?* She did.

The bird cage in the Melbourne Zoo was exactly like a bird cage – big and round, metal bars curving together at the top. Kate sang to the parrot that talked to her: ♫ *Only a bird in geelded cage.* A red smudge from the iron bars came off on the blouse she'd bought once in Italy.

Damn, thinks Kate, I've forgotten to bring the textbook I need to do my homework properly. It's not really homework, it's preparatory reading. The first lecture's in two weeks. She nearly told Richard she couldn't come with him this time because of the reading she wanted to do, and anyway it wasn't a good idea to keep Jessica out of the sixth form for the first week of the year. But it wouldn't have been fair to him. He's so responsible himself and loves getting cross when other people are irresponsible, like when they don't do their homework. Then he can square his shoulders under the burden, which is hard with his bull neck, but when he tries to do that Kate thinks he looks hilariously gorgeous.

If her stomach's better tomorrow she might go to the public library and see if they've got the book she needs. That would give Richard something to laugh about. Kate likes his chuckle. **The library? On holiday? You should go to the beach. You and Jessica should go to the beach, go on the ferry to Manly.**

Jessica has told him she hates the beach. Has done since she was eleven years old: get real, Dad. Who wants a tan these days, what are you, stuck in the sixties? All Jessica wants is to shop till she drops.

Richard comes back from breakfast. He checks again that he's thoroughly close-shaven. He looks for his conference pack. Jessica's using it as a lap table, writing postcards.

'When you're ready, Budgie,' he says. Without looking at

him, Jess holds the pack up. Jess hates it when he calls her that, but he's got off lightly this time: he must realise, for he blinks at Kate. She blinks back. Jessica rolls away over the fold-out bed to finish the cards with her head stuck under the dressing table. Richard picks up his jacket. As he strides out again he tells Kate to be ready by seven, it's dinner at the revolving restaurant and he wants her to sit next to the new president.

'Your new black dress is very elegant, wear that,' he says.

I'd rather wear the red one, she thinks.

At conferences, in the evenings, Kate is the parrot on the shoulder of a captain's jacket. *Awk.*

The menu is usually handwritten. In gold or green. Last night it said:

> *Medallions of kangaroo triumphant, presented on a*
> *cushion of raspberry coulis.*
> *Kebabs of buffalo, anointed with a blessing of garlic*
> *screened with a curtain of fennel.*

They farm buffalo in Australia! And serve it in restaurants! Kate expected it to taste like old dry wood but it absolutely melts!

Another wife, usually called Miranda, usually peers across the table through the shimmer of the candelabra and says brittle things about where she's travelled to lately. Last night, the Miranda was Beverley, one of the Australian wives. She said: *Deed you go to the Eenternational Meeting? Mexeeco Ceety was fabulous. The leather. Tooled leather. I came back laden. Belts, and bags, and a hat, a tooled leather hat! I'm going with Peter to the Paris meeting. Oh my God. Gucci.*

The captain's jacket said what it usually says at dinner parties: **Kate loved Italy but I had to keep her away from the silversmiths on the Ponte Vecchio ha ha.**

The men all said what they always say: **Ha ha.**

The women echoed: *Ha ha ha.*

It's the same every time. Except last night Kate decided to dance up and down on her captain's sloping rugby-thick shoulders, and talked about her Russian homework. That caused a crack in the brittle conversation.

Awk.

At least Martin Daney threw her a wink. Everyone else gave those slow nods that make their necks longer, so they looked like ducks peering into a bottle. But Martin laughed, with Kate and at everyone else. Martin's here without his wife. He's having a great time. His laugh drives Richard nuts. It always has, since they were in medical school together. Martin always comes off best, in everything Richard hopes he'll be best at. So Kate is careful not to laugh too much with Martin. She'd rather sit next to Martin tonight than Don Donovan the new president, who's weatherbeaten with a leer.

Two more days before they can go home.

Maybe her cold will be better tomorrow. Her stomach should be better. Kate won't go to the zoo, today or tomorrow. Jess is right. It's unfashionable to like zoos, to watch the beautiful creatures, caged and quietly angry with eyes that carry secret thoughts of everything and nothing, thoughts that are pure feeling, closed-off, secret. Today, Kate will go shopping and eat hot chips.

In the subway near the hotel is a place that sells the best hot chips in the world. Fat hot chips, salty. The best in the *universe*.

Salt's bad for her. It clogs her arteries. Mainly it's bad because if Richard sees her have salt, he does his big F.

She's bought hot chips every day and relished every grain of salt, ripping the bag open to lick in the corners. The stall keeper looks like one of his chips, square-set and nicely browned. He has a black moustache and white apron. He could be Russian. Maybe his name is Cyril, she thinks. Maybe his till is full of Russian coins.

*

Kate takes two Panadol and goes shopping until lunchtime. She buys more tissues for her cold. It's hell to have a cold in this hot weather, in the smog. She looks at all the shops she looked at yesterday. Then she goes underground. Cyril looks cross when he sees her. He has an excellent line in frowns, too; he and Richard could swap notes, thinks Kate. She wonders if he stalks round naked at home. A naked (saltless) hot chip. He might disapprove of her buying chips so often, even though it means more cash in his till. She raises on her toes to look over the counter, to see if the drawer has a section for Russian coins and squiggly links like the letter Z. Cyril gives her a very black look. Kate thinks she might have a temperature. Or maybe it's too many Panadol. She remembers to say thank you for the chips and sidesteps to the next stall for an avocado sandwich.

She walks through the underground arcade to the moving stairs that take her to the hotel. She holds the bag of hot chips to her chest. In the foyer, the Suitcase Boy glances at her. He can smell my chips, she thinks. In the lift she presses the button for floor nine.

The maid has cleaned the room. Jessica is long gone. Kate puts the safety chain across the door. She takes off her shoes. She takes off her blouse and her trousers. Then she takes off her underwear, except her knickers, and heaps all the pillows against the head of the queen-sized bed. She sits cross-legged in the middle of the mattress, leans back and tucks one heel into her crotch.

She lays the avocado sandwich on the quilt for later and opens up the bag of chips. Kate closes her eyes. Ah, Cyril, she breathes. My Katerina! he breathes back. The hot rising scent, deep, delicious. She eats the chips slowly, feeling the edges on her tongue.

*

The wide horizon stretches forever under the great grey bowl of the Russian sky. Katerina shivers as the icy wind cuts through her babushka. She does not shiver because of the cold. Nyet. She shivers because there in the distance are plumes of dust thrown up by the hooves of a huge black stallion galloping across the steppes. And on the stallion, spurring its sweating flanks, along with all the rest of it, towards her is – a hero, square-set, nicely browned?

Nyet! It is the young Crown Prince, Zukor! He has long ginger moustaches, a sabre in his hand, and lust in his heart for her, Katerina.

— Nyet, Zukor, she has cried again and again when he comes knocking on the door of her humble dacha. – I am a simple woman. I am old enough to be your aunt. I wish to live a modest life, I have no need for wealth, jewels, satin gowns.

But it has become harder and harder to keep the gurgling samovar between the hot-blooded Crown Prince and her own soft pliant form.

The stallion screeches to a halt. Its hooves scuff up the peaty soil of Mother Russia. Zukor flings himself at Katerina's feet. She clutches her babushka to her throat so he won't catch a glimpse of the milky white skin he so desperately wants to caress with his battle-roughened royal hands. He lays the sabre on the peaty soil between himself and Katerina. The stallion makes whatever noise enormous horses do when they're feeling excited and especially war-like.

— Come to my hunting lodge in Pvotsk, young Zukor begs. – I long to see your limbs on velvet sheets, to rub your gentle thighs with unguents from Bukhara.

— Nyet, says Katerina.

The royal moustaches tremble. The royal eyes are

moist with tears. The royal chest heaves. – Let me regale you with stirring tales of my war exploits, while we sip golden wine from Khazan and feast on grapes from sun-drenched slopes somewhere near the western suburbs of Constantinople. I will place Turkish delight in your sumptuous navel and lick it out again while outside, in the snow, maidens from Novgorod chant ritual mantras of great sexual power.

— Most definitely nyet, she says.

From the east, in the gathering darkness of the early-falling Russian night, gallops a nuggety brown pony. – A rival! exclaims Zukor. – Katerina, have you been false to me?

— I am true to myself, cries Katerina. – I want a simple life. All I want is to be moderately well-off.

The brown pony halts, rears, is reined in by its rider. Katerina's eyes meet those of the man on the nuggety brown pony. He has brown eyes like his steed, and no weapon except a chip basket. He has a black moustache.

The newcomer dismounts. Ignoring the Prince, he strides towards Katerina. – I come to claim my own, he says.

Cyril! Their hands meet, and cling, and start to fondle. The Crown Prince climbs back on his horse which looks as peeved as he does. He says sulkily, unhappily, – Anyhow, there's this really good story about the time I whacked the Mongols.

The stallion disappears into the distance. The brown pony discreetly turns its back while Katerina and Cyril sink down onto the welcoming soil of peaty Mother Russia. She thrusts aside her babushka. Cyril's moustache tastes salty, sleek. As she unties the laces at the neck of his black shirt, she sees his brown skin gleaming. She will roll against him, tumble and simmer; they will be chips seething in a – bed of oil?

Kate crumples up her Russian homework and eats the avocado sandwich. She'll cancel her enrolment at the language school, find something else to occupy the evenings while Richard's busy at his desk with one eye on his new agendas and the other on the Sky Sport channel of his personal 14-inch Sanyo. More of her Good Works committees? Maybe she could learn karate? No, Richard wouldn't like that. He'd think it meant she wanted to get into a situation where she'd have to use it. He'd laughed at her wanting to do Russian. Though he didn't flick an eyelid when she'd said once she might learn batik.

'I'll tell him I'm taking up aerobic pokerwork,' she says aloud and bites the sandwich crust. *Oh, Cyril . . .* 'Bloody hell, I can't even have a good fantasy. I always stop before the sexy bits.' Kate thinks it must be to do with her problem. That is, she has just one ambition:

✿ *to be the only faithful wife in the twentieth century* ✿

A beautiful ambition, Kate thinks. But no one else could ever admit that she's achieved it. Because if they are wives too, what would it say about them? And if they're husbands, what would it say about their wives? So it's a highly amusing ambition as well as beautiful, and she's pretty sure she's achieved it already. Though she'll have to wait until she's dead – or till Richard's dead – for it all to be validated, as it were.

She told Richard about her ambition, once. He didn't seem amused. He gave a Frown and went to make an urgent phone call to the regional cardiologist about a possible remit for the next big meeting.

'We're not that kind of people,' she had said even though she knew he wasn't listening. 'We're just not interested in affairs. I couldn't, could you? Getting used to new people's *bits* – I think it would be icky.' Even though he wasn't listening, his neck looked stunned that she would even mention it.

Kate thinks she was pretty daring too, to mention it. But

when she's really honest, as she always is when she talks to
Amelia and Libby, she confesses that she can't understand how
real people actually get to the stage where they're unfaithful.
Her sister and her best friend both look cross-eyed at that. So
Kate changes the subject. Because Kate thinks adultery should
happen only between book covers, not bed covers. Or in a
Technicolor escape for 90 mins, R16, put together by a director
with a Key Grip and outside locations. Kate realises adultery
can happen in the heart like that American president, the peanut one, said once. But that's fantasy, and no matter what the
Tenth Commandment says about coveting, fantasy never hurt
anyone. And Kate's never has been unfaithful even in her heart,
only with men like Cyril in her imagination and never got to
the sexy bits anyway, so yes, that means she has achieved her
ambition.

So where to go from here? thinks Kate.

To clamber off the bed and find more Panadol. She swallows two and then two more. Her stomach is pure cramping
hell again, but she'll be fine by tonight. She'd better be: there've
been enough Frowns this week. It's been a big agenda, poor
Richard. She takes some Coldrex too so she'll be able to smile
at the new president at dinner without her nose dripping into
the:

Cod and salmon in whitebait crême
with selected fresh herbs entwined on a futon of spinach.

'You look like Dracula's leftovers.' Jessica slings an armload of
bright plastic shopping bags onto the fold-out bed. At some
stage she's had her long brown hair tied in little pigtails all over
with coloured braid twisted into them.

'What do you call that?' asks Kate.

'Cool,' says Jess.

'I wish we'd done things like that when I was sixteen.' She

looks in the mirror. Jessica's right. The new black dress makes her face look hollow and the neckline is so prudent it's frightening. She pats rouge onto her cheekbones. Jessica laughs. Kate takes another look in the mirror. Yes, an early Colorama version of the Vampire's Bride. She laughs too, and dabs rouge on her nose. 'Bozo,' she says.

Jess rips open her parcels. A short black skirt, a purple tasselled scarf, a black wool cardigan, another short black skirt, a pair of red tights covered in black stars. 'I could've got all this back at St Lukes, for God's sake, but Dad'd be pissed if I didn't let him see I'm having a good time. After all, I'm missing school, I'd better show I'm grateful.' She flips a grin. 'What time're you and Dad going out? C'n I have room service? C'n I wait till you're gone and order what I like?'

'Sure,' says Kate. 'Just like last night. Dad'd be pissed if you didn't show him you're having a good time.' She drags the black dress over her head and hangs it back in the closet. She knew it was a good dress for a funeral, but she didn't want to look like the corpse herself.

'Wear the red one. Go on!' Jessica flops backwards on the double bed. 'What are you, a wimp or something?'

'Your father likes me to look suitable.' Kate puts her mouth into a prim curve; it makes her look like a Mother Superior, even in her low-cut size 14D cup. Jessica pretends to throw a pillow at her. Kate slips the gypsy dress on. At once she looks better – the colour matches the red dot on her nose. She washes her face, applies fresh make-up and lets Jess do her hair. Richard doesn't like her hair up and Kate knows that Jessica knows it. But Richard won't Frown if little Budgie's done it. So she murmurs *cheep*, which makes Jessica tap her shoulder with the hairbrush. Anyway Kate likes the way Jessica makes one thick brown curl fall down over her mother's shoulder.

Kate unfastens the top button of the bodice and considers the effect. Jessica jogs on the spot: her braids bounce around like mice tails. 'Cool, Mum. I reckon Dr Donovan fancies you. Give the old guy a thrill. Doesn't matter if he has a heart attack, there'll be plenty of specialists around.' Kate snorts: just as well the Coldrex has worked or she would have had to do her make-up a third time. Jessica dabs moisturiser on Kate's collar bones and down her sternum. The low neckline is astonishing. 'Watch out for Prof Daney too, eh? Oh, gross, though – who'd want to have an affair with a gynaecologist!' Kate ought to say 'Now' in a warning way, but the thought Jess has come up with is so appalling that Kate can only wish she'd said it first.

There is the rasp of a key in the keyhole. Richard pitches the door open and overarms his conference pack onto the bed.

He stands still for a second when he sees Kate. He can probably tell the dress isn't black – hard to know if it makes him Frown; he was Frowning already. Poor Richard, the timetable must have slipped.

Jessica hangs big twisted gold earrings on Kate's lobes. 'Isn't she gorgeous? C'n I have this dress when you grow out of it, Mum?'

Now Richard's Frowning at Jessica's hair. 'What are you trying to do to yourself?'

Jess grins and pats his bald head. 'Jealous are we, swee-tart?' She scrambles over the fold-out bed for the one unopened package and tosses it to Kate. 'Go on. Bought them for you.' Sheer black pantyhose with red and gold hand-painted flowers up the side. Outrageous. Gorgeous. Perfect.

'Haven't you got better things to spend your money on?' Richard wrestles into a clean shirt.

'Uh-uh.' Jessica shakes her head and turns on the TV. Soap-time: *Nay-ay-bours. Everybody needs good nay-ay-bours.*

Kate uncaps her bottle of Opium from duty free. She dabs some behind her ears and down her cleavage. A dab, too, behind each knee. Then she pulls on the new hose. They are sensually soft. Black and clinging. Mmmm, like Cyril's moustache.

chapter two

Satan howls. Kate shut him in the garage half an hour ago because her sister has come round. Everyone hates Satan, but he's Richard's dog. Richard's hardly ever home so Kate understands why it doesn't bother him that Satan's ten years old and has an intestinal problem.

'How long do dogs live? Can't you get a goldfish instead?' Amelia peers out the kitchen window. Satan, on his hind legs, squints through the garage window and bares his big brown teeth that match his big brown body. It's a smile: he loves Amelia.

'Don't let him see you. He'll shut up soon.' Kate drops two sachets of rosehip tea into the pot and sits at the colonial table. 'Have a bagel.'

'A bun with a hole in it.' Amelia doesn't seem impressed. 'Do they come in wholemeal?'

Kate pours the tea. It's good to be home. She loves her kitchen overlooking the side garden with its host of hibiscus and bougainvillaea, purple, orange and shocking pink. She loves the big staircase up to the kids' rooms and the main bedroom with its ensuite, and she loves the fact that Richard's got his own study down the far end of the house. She loves her sunroom, and the living room with its high stud and big main window and her piano, the Yamaha upright. She loves her new Bodum teapot too because you can see how dark the tea's getting without taking the lid off. Satan howls again, long and loud. She loves Satan too, really.

'You're a honey!' Amelia strokes the red bag, her present. 'I've never had a leather bag before! Only Mexican wool. Or jute bags from Trade Aid. Did you get it at a market?'

'Strand Arcade,' says Kate.

Amelia's nose gives a satisfied wrinkle. 'I don't even care if it's not environmentally sound.'

'We should kill all the cows anyway,' says Kate, 'they ruin the ozone layer.'

'And you brought me two presents!' Amelia holds the necklace across her forehead so she looks like a Hollywood version of Fatima in the harem and Kate feels a surge of admiration. Amelia's had small parts in TV shows, she's a speech therapist too one day a week, so she leads a frantically creative and useful life.

'I got something for Rebecca. D'you approve?' She pushes a little bag over the table.

Amelia peeps in. 'Eye make-up? She'll love it – ' She starts to smile, but the smile stops for a moment. Then, after a twitch at the corner of her mouth, the smile grows very wide, though Amelia tries to bite her lower lip to stop it.

'What?' asks Kate.

'Remembering when I was fourteen.' Amelia's hands are over her mouth now, still trying to hold the smile down.

'Give it here!' says Kate. 'I'll buy something else in Parnell and . . . '

'What's wrong?'

'I don't want 'Becca going the way you did.' Kate tries to snatch the package.

Amelia's smile bursts free. 'But 'Bec will love it. And there's no harm in it, not really, is there?'

'In what?' asks Kate. 'Exactly what?'

Amelia tips her head to one side. She gives a longing, yearning kind of pelvic moan.

Oh no, thinks Kate. The flicker in her older sister's eyes. The Bad-Girl-of-the-Family dreamy flicker. Kate's seen this flicker many times. Since Amelia began to wear make-up and have underage sex and go on to have far too much overage sex. 'Amelia. Not again.'

The moan comes again, entangled with a hungry kind of chuckle.

Oh God, thinks Kate. She sees the next few weeks will be full of many supportive pots of tea, many excitedly told intimate details. People are always falling in love with Amelia. So Amelia says. Every time, Kate hopes it's just the wishful thinking of the self-deluded. It never is. And it always ends in tears and in Kate saying earnest things to Amelia about marital fidelity. And last time, as she always does, Amelia swore faithfully to Kate that she'd be faithful to her little Barry, happy ever more.

Kate sighs. 'Who is it this time, Scatty-Rat?'

'Oh, hon. When you were away. That drama weekend at Howick – ' Amelia's eyes go vague, more faraway. 'God, talk about intense – all those imaginative people – we all *bonded*, Kate, so *deeply*. The *energy*. People got really *into it*.' Amelia's staring right through Kate. 'The movement tutor, hon – my God, his torso – Drystan can *ripple*, like a *snake*!' Amelia starts to tell all. He got so into it, he wanted to sleep with her.

'That's a very misleading expression.' Kate grips her tea mug. It's hopeless, she thinks, how come Amelia's so different from me?

'But Kate – get this – I didn't!' Amelia smiles in triumph.

Kate's heart leaps: a happy ending? 'Good for you!'

'I nearly did,' says Amelia. 'But then I thought – no. Not this time. I really wanted to, hon, but like you said, I've got to try. I should. For Barry's sake. I do love my wee husband.'

Barry is very short. It could be quite cute, in bed with Barry, Kate thinks, like having a cuddle with the Wobbly Man, if you were into that sort of thing. The Wobbly Man and Big

25

Ears. Little Noddy. 'You used to be crazy about Enid Blyton books.' Kate couldn't help saying that, though she wouldn't hurt Amelia for the world. Her sister looks puzzled for a moment, then clutches the leather bag to her breasts.

'Oh, Kate, I know what you think, but Kate – Drystan is gorgeous!'

Kate grasps her mug again and opens her mouth to say fortifying things about the ways of faithfulness. But the orange Bad Girl light is hot in Amelia's big brown eyes.

'It's all right for you. You and Richard are so happy, you dance together like a dream, you go away with him, and you've got two cars. Barry's off up north for another fortnight soon.'

Kate has a peculiar feeling under her ribs. It will be the same old story, no matter what Amelia's said. Adultery, in the flesh. Naked thighs and closed curtains in the middle of the day. Twisted, sweat-soaked sheets and straining limbs. Desire, hot tongues, heaving breasts. Just like in the movies. How danger-ous, how exciting – how awful. 'An aerobics person won't make you happy. You're only in it for the – physical. I'm sure that's not enough. Honestly, you're always sorry in the end.'

'But you and Richard have everything.' Amelia holds the red bag to her face and sniffs it: new leather, environmentally unsound, aah. 'God, it smells so much better than jute. If bloody Barry didn't spend a fortune on his car I could afford real leather for myself.'

Kate pictures Barry in his 1960 V8, which he's restored. He's put blocks on the pedals so he can reach them. 'If only Barry knew! He's so proud of you, Amelia, and you let him down! How can you say your marriage is working when you let yourself be driven by – other people's rippling muscles?'

Satan howls.

'Of course you wouldn't understand,' Amelia says. 'Maybe you do have everything, hon. But I bet you still haven't had an orgasm.'

'I wish Satan would shut up,' says Kate.

'No, really, Kate, it's getting serious. Listen, I know this fantastic naturopath over in Ponsonby who . . . '

'I have,' says Kate. 'I think.'

'Then what's it like?' asks Amelia. Now her look says: *How can you bear to live without knowing what it's like, Kate? And you're married to a doctor, Kate! And Kate, believe me, nothing is more glorious and wonderful than –*

'I'm perfectly content,' says Kate, doing a conscious mental dodge to shut Amelia up and change that maddening glint in her eye before it makes Kate explode. 'I've never even wanted another man. I'm very unlike you.'

But Amelia points at her. 'You're over forty, hon. Life's passing you by. It would do you good to leap into bed with an aerobics instructor on the off chance you'd find out what I'm talking about. Oh, all right, it's different for you. You don't like adventures. Not real ones.'

'You think I'm dull.' Kate spits the words. 'Because I didn't have platoons of men before I got married like you did. But I'm perfectly happy and I don't want a platoon now.'

Amelia grins. 'I can't help it if I'm more highly sexed than you.' She scoops up her presents and the eye make-up. 'And if I want an affair with Drystan, I'll have it. The real reason I haven't started yet is not because of Barry – I want to lose some weight first, that's all.' She sweeps out with a rich, deep-pelvised laugh.

Kate is furious. She doesn't need her sister to upset her. She doesn't need an orgasm. Amelia drives off and Satan barks to show his thwarted passion. 'Shut up!' yells Kate. 'Shut up!'

Evening sun slants over the garage. Kate ought to shout at Jessica to get off the phone and let Satan out for a run before Richard gets home. But the kitchen door is shut and her hands are covered in

Italian meatball mixture. For the however–many–days–it–is–in–the–six–years–they've–lived–here, Kate thinks about getting the downstairs phone moved to the kitchen. But there wouldn't be room for the answerphone as well, not with the coffee perc and grinder and the microwave and food processor and the mini–grill and all the marvellous pottery they've collected since they could afford the quality stuff. And the answerphone's essential, for all Richard's messages, not to mention hers from all the Good Works committees she's meant to be on.

Outside there's a rumble and slither. Kate looks at the clock. Seven? Too early for Richard, but that's the double garage door doing its automatic opening. The Mazda MX5 comes gunning up the drive.

Kate boots the kitchen door with her foot. 'Jessica! Dad's home!'

A yelp and giggle, the phone slapped down, and Jessica's sitting on the colonial bar-stool next to the microwave, saying, 'What c'n I do to help, Earth Mother? Goddess of My Clean Socks and Neatly Pressed School Blouses?'

'Empty the dishwasher and start loading it again. And tell your father about your history mark.'

'D'I have to?' But it's just a mutter. Kate rinses her hands and sets the skillet on the stove. Jessica's already whisking through the clean dishes and stacking the machine again. She is a wonderfully efficient young person when she cares to be.

Richard stands in the doorway, filling it up with his shoulders and his burly neck. 'Who was on the phone. Need I ask.' He isn't asking: they're not questions, anyway. Jessica grins at him through her tangle of brown, gelled curls.

'She got 90% on the rebellion of something. It was a snap test and she's only been at school three days,' says Kate. She knows that both she and Jess are expecting to hear: **Not bad, what happened to the other 10%? Ah well, you're just my little budgie brain.**

'Not bad.' Richard loosens his tie. 'Pity about the other 10%. You've made your mother waste her time over dinner,' he tells Jessica. 'I've been trying to call. We're going out with Helco. Virtue, eight o'clock.'

'You've put the car away,' says Kate.

'It's time I drove yours. Check how it's running,' says Richard. Kate keeps her mouth shut. She had her Mitsubishi Chariot serviced just before they went to Sydney.

'Well, I've still got to eat.' Jessica tears some plastic wrap to put over the meatballs. 'I'll pig out on some nachos — where's the corn chips?'

'Make enough for Owen,' says Richard. 'I passed him on the main road. God knows I've had a rough enough time trying to organise my day. I hardly need the Great Mistake as well.' It used to be a good joke: *roar*, **My first two are twins, it was a great mistake to do it twice in one night.**

Chuckling, Richard leaves the kitchen. They hear him run up the stairs, the main bedroom door is slammed, then there's the noise from the water cylinder that means the shower in the ensuite is turned on full.

Kate used to think that boys and fathers should get on well. But it isn't always true. **Don't baby him, he's old enough and ugly enough to do things for himself. Kate, have you finished my tax return yet?**

Jessica has found the sour cream and Kate has taken a can of chilli beans out of the pantry. 'I'll do it, Mum. Go and get changed. You'd wow 'em like that, but I don't think Virtue's quite the place.' Kate's wearing an old shirt of Richard's over lycra tights.

'Pity,' says Kate. 'What does Owen want?' She's curious. Also worried. Owen doesn't come home during the week. He works in a menswear store just off Queen Street. Richard's never worn the silk tie Owen bought him with his first pay. At least he has a job, Kate thinks, and at least he can support himself now. Heavens, not all doctors' sons want to continue the family tradition and Richard's own father was a small-town livestock auctioneer; where's the tradition in that? The other twin, Alice, has gone to Christchurch where she'll do superbly well in a journalism course. She was lucky to be taken without a full degree, it seems. Everyone else there already has one or even two. But she, at only twenty, youngest in the group, has won prizes for photography as well as for an essay on Why Auckland is the Most Go-ahead City in the Pacific Ring of Fire. Richard is impressed by Alice's brain, but Kate knows he'd rather it were Owen's.

There's the squeak and rattle-thump of a bicycle being propped up in the porch. And a bark, whimper and whine. Richard had let Satan out of the garage.

'F'Christ's sake, Satan, get in behind!' That's Owen's joke. He and Alice named Satan. Richard wanted to call the meat-coloured dog Bonaparte – because that's what he'd do to bones with that jaw – but the twins stuck with their choice. Kate finds it hugely useful when Jehovah's Witnesses come door-knocking: *You're wasting your time. Satan! Come here, Satan.*

Paws scrabble on the front door, then come skidding and pounding through the house to end up on Jessica's shoulders.

'It is such a drag to be loved by someone that stinks!' yells Jessica. 'One fart and you're back in the garage!'

Kate uses both arms full strength to make Satan sit, and both hands full strength to haul a new dog-roll from the fridge. She cuts a six-inch piece which Satan downs in three gulps.

'Can I have a lager?' Owen, tall and wiry, stands next to his mother. The Sydney braces that she bought are handsome against his chambray shirt. He twists a hand into the lock of hair he's trained to fall over his forehead. 'And can you hug me, too?' Something in his eyes says he's two years old, not twenty. Kate puts both arms, full strength, around her son and squeezes. Jessica comes up too and winds her arms round the pair of them.

'Dad didn't like me working at Pageant, anyhow,' says Owen. 'So he won't be mad that I've been made redundant.'

Oh shit! thinks Kate. She hugs Owen so he won't be able to see her face. Jess takes a bottle of Mac's Gold out of the fridge, pops the cap, and holds it out.

'Cheers.' Owen keeps one arm round Kate while he up-ends the bottle into his mouth. 'I might have to live back home, if that's OK.'

'You're not having your old room,' says Jessica. She's hugging again, tighter now. 'And say anything rancid about my friends when they come over, and you're dog-roll.'

Kate is in front of her wardrobe wondering what the Helco people would find appropriate, and why it's important to be appropriate anyway. Is it a big drug company, or just a new one? She can't remember. She also wonders when to tell Richard about Owen.

Richard, in socks and skants, pats aftershave on his upper lip, chin and throat, smoothes the remnants of his hair, black and shiny around the back of his head. He's taking a lot of notice of his own appearance tonight. His scalp is nicely brown-pink – The Barometer reads reasonably good mood. He hasn't been grumpy all week – no more than usual. He was alarmingly full of bounce and jokes for a few weeks early in the year, which the kids hated. When Alice flew to Christchurch, just before they left for Sydney, the last thing she said was, 'I'm not coming home till Dad's normal again.' Well, he's normal now, after those terrible few days in the hotel. He glances at Kate with a normally preoccupied small-f-frown. 'Is my grey suit back from the cleaners?'

It's still in a heap in the back of the Chariot, so Kate can honestly say no. She decides to wear black evening trousers and the purple shirt she bought in the Queen Victoria Building.

She'll wear silver and onyx cockerel earrings, and her silver and onyx bangles. As she's doing up her buttons, she stares at Richard, sideways at the full-length mirror, pulling in his stomach and tightening his buttocks. He runs a hand over his chest.

'Squash,' he says. 'I'd have time for that, two or three times a week. Wouldn't I.'

He played once before they went to Sydney and came home very late and very uplifted with himself, although exhausted. *Squash?* It's for idiots still under thirty, as far as Kate can see. It's torn ligaments and heart attacks for the mid-forties like Richard. 'You'll never have time for that, darling. If you want to get fit, walk your dog now and then.' She smiles, though: he does look delicious, posing and turning to see his own behind. 'I haven't seen you prink like that since we were being illicit, pre-twins.' She crosses to him and runs her own hands over his chest, the wiry black hairs, the firm pebbles of his nipples, up behind his neck to the thick pad of muscle that made him such a good player in the Varsity A team twenty years ago. Well, a fairly good player, if she's being honest. 'You're still fit enough for me, Rrrr–ichard.'

He gives a quick blink and reddens beneath the eyes. With the twitchy sexy swagger that makes her laugh, he puts one hand firmly behind her waist, offers his other hand with a flourish, and they're waltzing *one two three, one two three* round the bedroom. They do their deepest dip, then another, and *one two three* into his super-wonderful chassez reverse turn. As they whirl to a stop, Richard puts both hands on her waist and lifts her easily even though in her high heels she's exactly as tall as he is. He pops her down again. 'I could do to lose some weight,' he says.

'My champion, to do that in your socks!' Still laughing, Kate sits at her dressing table: he'll lose weight without trying when he learns about Owen. He'll be so mad he'll spend the next week arguing the case over dinner, pushing his food around, forgetting to put any in his mouth. She won't tell him till they're back home, so he can put on a good face to Helco. He's hoping to get money from them for travel or something to further his gastro-intestinal research, some study or other that the hospital refuses to pay for. Richard's always upset because he's never got money from anywhere, while academics like Martin Daney always do. Richard tries so hard, it really isn't fair, thinks Kate.

He's still red under the eyes. 'Er – nice.' He nods at the purple shirt.

'It cost a fortune.'

He grunts, in a way that says *good*, and asks her to pour him a whisky since she's ready first. And get the spare keys to her car: he won't carry them on his ring, it makes it far too heavy with his work keys as well.

'Amelia was on about losing weight.' She slides the onyx bangle on. 'I know she's going to have another affair. God, she gets under my skin sometimes. Darling – do you – ' She wants to ask if Richard thinks an orgasm would be worth it. But it's difficult. He'd wonder why she didn't ask him twenty years ago. Except she didn't know about them then.

But Richard's still trying to square his shoulders, flexing one of his biceps. It must be really important to impress the Helco people, she thinks as she goes to pour the whisky: better give the poor love a double.

chapter three

Kate and Richard drive round the waterfront to Virtue. His mouth is set in a peculiar expression. Conference dinners are all the same, and drug company dinners are all the same too, but it's a different same. Everyone will grip gins and tonics, especially the drug reps, though they'll only pretend to drink because they're on the job. Kate won't pretend, she'll need all the help she can get. And it won't matter if she has too much, there'll be lemon slices in the gin, for vitamins

She glances at Richard as he parks the Chariot. Fidgety expression, still. All the medical-surgical persons will wear funny expressions. They don't look like that when the drug companies give out the diaries and ballpoint pens and jotter pads, she thinks. Only if there's a sniff of travel money. Must be for a trip to a Universal Congress of all the possible Inter-related-Ologists.

Clinging to her g&t she will listen, watch. The medical persons will stand in groups and swivel so their words shoot straight at the nearest rep. The reps will be like circling aircraft tracked by ack-ack guns.

The ophthalmologists, neurologists and orthopaedic specialists will fire: '*My lecture at the University of Stockholm . . .* ', '*My communication in the latest* BMJ *. . .* ', '*With all my clinical experience in Kiev . . .* '

The ack-ack will get louder as the g&ts get low: '*In my

well-received keynote address at . . .', '*My last lead article in the* Lancet . . .*', '*I was the first New Zealander for a damn long time, y'know . . .*'

The cardio-thoracic surgeons will have their hearts upon their sleeves. The neurosurgeons will tremble with anticipation. The geriatricians will lean against the bar. Whatever they say will be the same as always. Whatever they say will really mean: *I'm an expert in my field and my insight is superb. But I ought to let you know – just on the quiet – that:* **I'm quintessentially modest. Humble, too.**

And poor Richard never gets a chance. It makes Kate mad: the public simply don't realise how hard it is being on the ear-piece end of a stethoscope. Sometimes he does get trapped in all the one-upmanship but though it's maddening, it's totally understandable. He seems particularly on edge now – he reaches for the door handle and fumbles a little as he finds it. Putting his shoulders very straight, he ushers her into the restaurant. Kate recognises many faces from the local hospitals. Don Donovan, new president of whatever-the-heck-Associ-ation of Somethings is over from Australia. He really gets around. Jeffries is up from Hamilton.

The usual type of young woman drug rep with long blonde hair, who is usually called Kylie, gives Richard a smile and Kate a g&t. Kate says thank you. 'Pleased to meet you, Mrs Wild-burn,' says the Kylie. 'I'm Brianne.' She walks away to offer other gins.

Richard nudges Kate and indicates another Helco person, late-forties with a moustache and sandy hair. 'Marketing manager. Sit next to him at dinner if you can. I don't want to be too obvious, Kate, so do your stuff.'

Awk, bob, nod and ruffle your pinions. Kate gives him an I-get-fed-up-with-all-this look, and sips her gin. There's tension in the slope of Richard's shoulders as he moves to talk to the marketing manager. The man has a nice open face –

perhaps he honestly believes that Helco does a good job. Ah well, we all need drugs, thinks Kate with an appreciative sip of her gin. She takes a bigger sip so the lemon won't be wasted.

By the time Kate's glass is empty the marketing man's still with Richard and so is the young woman rep with swinging blonde hair. Brianne? That's new, thinks Kate. There's probably a male one called Pagett, or Perrin or — A young man rep in a super-trendy suit puts a fresh glass in her hand. 'I'm Marsden,' he says. 'Mars Ridley-Dwight. And you?' Kate does the small talk. She's grateful for the new slice of vitamins; there's a sprig of mint as well.

She glimpses Viv Lingate between two groups of swivelling surgeons. Viv wears the usual look of all the spouses at these evenings: *I'm here because I'm here because I'm here*. Kate catches Viv's eye. They've had coffee together a few times. Viv winks. Marsden's off to fill her glass as well.

Kate realises the marketing manager is beside her. There's a tiny grin on his face; maybe he's seen the look between Kate and Viv. His sandy hair, the humorous set of his eyes, and her first gin downed too fast. And do your stuff, Kate, Richard said. So, 'What's a nice guy like you doing in a job like this?' she asks.

'Someone's gotta do the doity woik,' he says, so quietly that for a moment she can't believe she heard him right. His moustache whiffles.

And her laugh bursts out. 'Hard labour?'

'Another gin?' He says it *geen*. Australian. But her second one's still half full so he takes one himself from a passing Marsden or Brianne. He's really drinking, not pretending; a confident, charming man, thinks Kate.

Richard seems to be charming too at dinner, down the other end of the table. Kate's managed to sit next to the Helco man, so Richard's head is smooth above the u-shaped rim of his hair. Thank goodness she hasn't told him about Owen yet. He has a new joke. Probably another operating theatre, blood and gory bits kind. Kate hears Viv Lingate and Greta Daney making him repeat it. *Ha ha, oh oh oh!* That's nice – she doesn't want him as light-hearted as he was in January but along with his good temper went more energy in bed for a week or so. He took a little longer over things, which made Kate begin to feel – well, interesting. She'll never let on to her sister. Is there something she could read about orgasms over forty? She found a book once which recommended a particular exercise called a Kugel; she's been practising it whenever she remembers but nothing's happened yet. Sydney was a disaster of course, but Kate wonders if the interesting side of things might start up again now they're home. She knows there must be more to sex than she's discovered so far, otherwise why would people like Amelia find it irresistible?

She sees Martin Daney laughing. Would what Jessica suggested, an affair with a gynaecologist, be useful after all? For research purposes, of course.

You can justify anything in the name of research

thinks Kate. A joke of my own! **Ha ha** and *ha ha ha*.

Kate knows she's being insubordinate. She ought to be bobbing up and down, the parrot on the captain's jacket. She should be awking to the Helco man. God, what's his name? Helco makes surgical and dental supplies – she's forgotten the details, though Richard told her in the car. How can she impress the man for Richard's sake? But at the moment he's fending off a thoroughly subtle barrage of humility from Jeffries on his other side, so she shrugs and pokes her entrée fork at the raw venison fillet. She's not very hungry after that bagel which rhymes with Kugel with Amelia.

Tom Lingate's two down, on the other side of short-skirted Brianne. Kate's heard rumours about that man. She wonders if Viv knows. She heard a rumour about Viv once too. She didn't believe it, though.

Tom leans forward as if he senses her thinking about him, and winks. He eyes her purple shirt. The idea of having an affair with an anaesthetist has a gross side, too – I mean, thinks Kate, would you notice? She tries not to laugh.

Viv Lingate has a hand on Don Donovan's chest now, tapping him and talking lightly as his leer shifts back and forth. Tom must have given her instructions too, thinks Kate, he's probably keen to get on the committee of the All-World Surgical What's-its.

Brianne turns to Kate at last, rattling her fake gold bangles. The young thing's far too thin, thinks Kate, she should go home to her mum for a good honest feed. 'So nice to meet you, Mrs Wildburn. We think it's vital to have the wives at these dinners. It must be so difficult for you to keep up with what's happening in the profession.'

Kate can't think what to say – has this person heard of Women's Lib? But then the nearest Kate herself ever came to being feminist was buying a copy of *Broadsheet* once. She found it incomprehensible. She would have felt politically incorrect to throw it out so she slipped it in the Donations to the Crippled Children bin at the shopping mall.

The rep's still smiling. 'What about husbands keeping up with what their wives do?' asks Kate. 'Sauce for the goose.'

The drug rep blinks. 'But saving lives is so important, isn't it?' Flipping her long hair, she turns back to Tom. Is she really a drug rep, or a Groupie for the Operating Theatre? thinks Kate: Brianne should start a club – Bimbos for Surgery, what a lovely thought!

Kate still isn't hungry. But the wine is good. A Coonawarra red. When she's poured more for herself she offers it to the marketing manager. 'An' what's a nice goil like you doin' inna place like dis?' he asks from the corner of his mouth like a B movie gangster. An accomplice, another fifth columnist! They both laugh. Richard sends her a tentative checking-things-out smile.

'Well, why did you get into drugs?' she asks the Helco man. 'If I can put it that way?'

'I stopped believing in my plane,' he says.

'What on earth do you mean?'

He tells her he used to do top dressing in Australia.

How marvellous. A thoroughly convincing reason for taking a job as a marketing manager. 'Over ranches full of kangaroos?'

'Only if I got my co-ordinates wrong.' He has a deep chuckle which she finds contagious. Richard looks more relaxed when she takes another glance his way. They continue talking, about the outback where Kate's never been, about wombats and emus. He says he's crazy about the parrots. He doesn't ask why she starts to laugh again, just smiles and pours more wine. But he does believe in his work now, he says, and she sees it's true. After all, no matter how ghastly these dinners can be, the world needs Panadol and Coldrex, thinks Kate, and whatever-it-is-that-Helco-makes.

She waves to Richard across the potatoes and asparagus, and he waves back. The main course of smoked ox tongue tastes exquisite, she's hungry after all.

By the time dessert is served, Richard has changed places with her and is his amusing, happy-smiling best.

'Lovely view,' says Kate to Greta Daney and Viv Lingate. The lights on the harbour, a dark satin sky, enough moon to see the cone of Rangitoto over the water. So beautiful it makes Kate want to cry.

'Lovely,' agrees Greta and Viv waggles her empty wine glass.

'How's the job?' Kate asks. 'Still one day a week at your local medical centre?'

'I like a routine,' says Greta. 'And it helps me buy my clothes.'

Kate remembers that the Daney boys must both be off to

boarding school this year. Greta will be bereft, like Richard's mother was when he went off to school: St Kents was the best for my only chick of course, says Richard's mother, sighing. Kate would like to give Greta a little hug but she doesn't know her well enough. 'It must be tough to have your boys away,' she says.

'It's tougher having Martin on his own,' Greta explains. 'The children help to spread him out.'

She's pretending she doesn't really mind, thinks Kate, how cool and brave she is. Kate's sure she'd like Greta very much if she had the chance. Greta always looks immaculate. Once Kate heard the Dean of Surgery call her a Rose in Full Bloom, but Kate found that rather strong; she's more like that what-you-call-it that flowers in winter, hellebore, the Winter Rose. Which, according to Amelia and Barry who know about those things, is a useful purgative. Anyway Greta's the perfect image of the doctor's wife: short, frosted hair, matching bags and shoes. Discreet little pearls in her ears. Kate knows the silver cockerels dangling from her own lobes aren't at all the thing. That suits her fine. They're fighting cockerels, after all. Maybe she could find some tiny silver hand grenades, that would be even less suitable.

Viv Lingate asks, 'What's your latest, Kate? Still Saving Orphans of various kinds, and Preventing Cruelty to Extinct Species?'

Viv has short thick brown hair, very smooth and neat too, but her mouth's wide and full-lipped and there's often a wicked spark in her eye. They've had some really good gossips. Kate knows Viv would understand about Owen.

'How do you tell a husband something that's sure to upset him?' asks Kate.

Greta looks alarmed, but Viv huddles down excitedly. Tom Lingate comes to hear the gossip too, bending over Kate's chair. 'Don't blurt to Richard till I've had a chance,' she warns Tom, and tells them about Pageant, and how she has to choose the moment so Richard won't be too upset.

'Can't understand you women.' Tom reaches for the wine bottle. 'He's grown up, he can take it. I'll tell him, if you like.'

'You dare!' says Viv. Tom pretends to be afraid and hides behind Kate.

'How was Sydney?' he says in her ear.

Kate takes a deep breath. Can she say how awful Richard was? 'Well – what are you like at conferences?'

'Free booze,' mutters Viv. 'He's into all he can get.'

Greta sits back, immaculate, poised and pale. 'Martin's noisier than ever. That's why I never go. I've been most places anyway, by now.' She turns her perfectly groomed head at the sound of her husband, who roars with laughter as usual as he leans over the marketing manager's shoulder. Kate hopes Richard's made headway about that travel money: she hadn't mentioned it to the man, how could she? She also wonders if this month Richard will speak to Martin about her bad periods.

Kate confides to Greta, Viv and Tom that Sydney was a disaster. 'It always is,' says Viv. Kate tells them about the mud-dled sleeping arrangements, and how sick she was and says, at last, how grumpy Richard was.

'But look at him now,' says Viv. Greta nods and smiles. He's telling his joke again. The manager urges him to repeat it to the blonde rep, who makes her eyes go wide and beckons Marsden hyphen-Dwight. *Ha ha ha* and **ha ha ha**.

Kate hears Martin say something jolly to Richard about having a round of golf sometime, and coming for a sail. Richard's neck thickens. Richard and Kate don't have a boat.

By the end of dessert and after an espresso, Kate's squiffy because of the g&ts and the wine as well as two excellent brandies. She gives an I've-had-enough nod to Richard but he ignores it. Maybe he hasn't had good vibrations from Helco after all, maybe he's still hoping. She wishes the Daneys hadn't come tonight; Martin, being in obstetrics, is in a glamour part of the profession. There's no romance about Richard's guts and bowels.

The token female specialist and her husband have gone, and so has everyone except the Lingates and the Daneys. The marketing man's still easy-going and alert, but blonde Brianne hides her mouth behind a hand and her jaw stretches. The other Helcos have been allowed to go. 'Let's move to the bar,' says Kate. 'It'll be easier for the waiter-persons. They'll want to get the tables ready for tomorrow.' The marketing man stands up but everyone else seems bewildered. 'I know how tired Alice gets, waitressing,' explains Kate. Darling Alice so far away in Christchurch, trying to find work to help out with her student fees.

Kate and the Helco man sit up on the bar-stools. The bar tender's trying not to yawn too. She makes a little face at him and he gives a silent laugh.

The others follow, slowly. Climbing onto the stool seems tricky for Tom but he holds his whisky steady. 'Alice? Going to be a beauty. Like her mum.' He's slurring. Viv rolls her eyes at Kate again.

'I miss her so much,' says Kate. 'I'm trying not to but I do, so much it hurts.'

'Hell, couldn't wait to get mine off.' Martin gives his full-throated laugh and Richard winces. 'Greta'd turn them into wimps, she organises the hell out of them because I won't let her do it to me.' He laughs again. 'If they've got to be organised, it'll be at a boarding school where they can take it out on other kids without their mother fussing.'

'Alice is fine, do her good to get away.' Richard drains his glass. 'And little Jessica — get this — scored 95% in the latest school exam for history. Following in the Brain's footsteps, eh.'

It was a class test, and it was 90%, thinks Kate. God, we should go home.

'And the Great Mistake is up for store manager,' says Richard. 'He'll make it to the top before too long.' Oh do shut up, thinks Kate.

Tom Lingate makes a noise like a bark. Viv nudges him. 'Bloody hell, he's got a right to know,' says Tom. Viv punches Tom's arm so he spills his drink. 'The women are keeping it from you, mate. Your boy's been made redundant.'

Richard's jaw drops. He looks at Kate as if someone's hit him on the head with his own sigmoidoscope. Mind you, thinks Kate, that's less of a shock than his patients get when he uses it on their other ends. Damn, this is all his fault. I wanted to leave an hour ago. 'Darling, that's why he came home to-night. He's not with Pageant any more.'

The bar tender surreptitiously pours Kate another brandy. There are murmurs of concern from the Helco people. Viv pats Richard, soothing, *there there there.*

' Ah, he'll get a payment,' says Richard once his jaw's under control. 'That'll be a cushion while he gets more work.'

Kate is squiffy. But Owen's been getting $7.50 an hour, so $300 a week. It's normal to get a certain percentage of a week's pay for each year's service, though she doesn't know what the situation is for a shop assistant. 'He's only been there six months. If he gets even $150, he'll be lucky.'

The Helco manager gives Kate a sympathetic smile. 'A lot of employers specify a full year's service before they pay out. Money's a bastard. Risky times.' How nice he is, thinks Kate. I should remember his name for next time – John?

They slip down from the bar-stools and say goodnight. Greta kisses Richard while Martin kisses Kate. Greta and Kate kiss Tom, and Richard and Martin kiss Viv, and Viv pats Richard again. No one kisses John, though everyone shakes his hand. A pilot's hand.

43

'Let's have lunch sometime,' says Kate to Greta. 'You too, Viv?'

'Yes, let's,' they say.

As Kate and Richard go out into the cool night air, Richard's shoulders look wider than the shape of Rangitoto in the dark night sky. The top of his head's gone brick-red as if he's a Rangitoto thinking about erupting after lying dormant for several hundred years.

'He'll get another job,' says Kate. 'It might take time, but . . . '

'Did John say anything to you?' asks Richard. 'About Madrid? Hell, I could use that trip. The contacts. God, if bloody Academic Daney gets it, it'll be the last nail for my research. Did you know he's boasting about getting his century? One hundred papers published? Huh. All talk. He's such a bloody showman, no performance. It's high time I got something that I want.'

chapter four

Kate's off to her very best friend Libby's for a quick sandwich. She hasn't given Lib her Sydney earrings yet, but Libby's flat out with designs for a decorating job and hasn't time for a proper lunch out, chatting. So Kate runs into the Remuera deli, buys croissants and brie and tomato salad and runs out into the street where she sees Greta Daney near the chemist's. You meet everyone in The Village sooner or later.

'You're looking well,' says Kate. And she does, in the unexcited way that Kate finds so intriguing.

'I'm off for a few days,' says Greta. Kate thinks she must be going to see her boys for there's a faint glow in her cheeks. Greta opens her package and shows Kate a lilac spongebag with a matching make-up satchel. 'To Spain, next week. Ten days in Madrid. One of the few perks of being married to a prof,' she says with a tinkly laugh, 'you can hardly turn it down.'

'I thought you'd been everywhere,' says Kate, thinking God, not Martin, no!

'I've never been to *Spain* – ' Greta tips her head, sideways then back, as if she hears the strum of a mandolin: tip! tip! 'Maybe if Martin's just observing, if he doesn't have to give a talk, he won't be quite so manic. And it's a chance to get away. The rat race, it's so tedious.' She gives an amused, bored lift of one eyebrow. Kate doesn't feel very sympathetic but she manages an understanding nod.

'And Spain – I have a passion for classical guitar, Kate. I can't resist. It's so – stirring.' Kate can't imagine Greta being stirred by anything. Greta gives a cool, poised smile and glances at a neatly typed list she carries headed: THINGS TO DO. 'Must fly,' says Greta. 'Bye.'

Oh Richard! thinks Kate as she watches Greta walk immaculately away, Richard, I am sorry!

chapter five

Monday, and Kate's rushing before she helps with Meals on Wheels. She has to go to the mall and visit – oh, hell, what?

- The dry cleaners, with Richard's dark blue blazer, which he hasn't been able to wear as it's astonishingly crumpled.
- A shoe shop, because Satan has eaten one of her black evening high-heels.
- The sports store? Right, new sweat bands for Richard because the ones she bought last week are too tight. He's back to being grumpy. He's played squash on Tuesdays and Thursdays and comes home disgustingly late, totally walloped some nights and smug-faced and bouncy (though managing to be grumpy too, he's multi-talented) on others. He is losing weight. She's not sure whether it's from squash or rage about Martin Daney.
- The library, for a biography of Beethoven because she hasn't had a good cry for a while.
- The post office to send a letter to Alice, who she's still missing horribly.
- The second trip to the supermarket this week: Big Fresh where they have the funny *papier mâché* figures singing, milking cows to show how fresh the milk is, and catching marlin in a tiny dinghy above the fish counter. Now that Owen's home they empty entire tubs of peanut butter in

less than five days. She'd forgotten how much a skinny male person could eat. But she doesn't mind how often she visits Big Fresh: she loves the songs and has to stop herself from singing along out loud.

* And a bookshop for the latest *Auckland Enquirer* because they have marvellous headlines and she's making a collection:

Birkenhead Grandmother Pregnant with Hitler's Ghost-Child
He kept his boots on 71-year-old complains

The dry cleaner's first. The assistant pats the blazer pockets and fishes out a piece of white paper. 'S'this something you want?'

She takes it, but doesn't unfold it till she's walking past the bargain table just inside the shoe shop. She expects it to be a lab slip, with scribbled numbers that mean Freddie Johnson's ESR's too high or Bessie Chartwell's urine is too acid. But:

```
Glade Motor Inn
Tui Grove Greenhithe
dble   $118.00 (inc. GST)
13/2    pd cash
```

'Can I help you?' asks a woman in a white blouse and black skirt, smiling.

'I'm going to sit down,' says Kate. The display shelves with all the shoes are swooping towards her then away again. She feels the woman's hand under her arm as she's guided backwards into a chair. 'Give me a minute,' says Kate.

She folds the invoice in half, then into half again, and again, and a fourth, fifth, sixth time. No matter how big a piece of paper you start with, you can't fold it more than that. Someone told her once, and now she knows it's true. She unfolds it. It still isn't a lab slip. What an immediately suspicious mind she's got. But then again. Cash. For a motel? There's never been a conference at Greenhithe – has there? *Greenhithe*? Not in February, 13/2. And Richard wouldn't stay the night in Greenhithe, it's only a few minutes out of town. And he wouldn't pay cash, he's too proud of his Gold Card. 13/2, some weeks ago. Five weeks. She can't work out what day, she'd need a calendar, she can't think.

Someone else must have put this in Richard's pocket. He must have picked it up as a piece of rubbish, and put it in his own pocket. But Richard never picks up rubbish. He must have thought it was a lab slip. Richard must have paid for someone who lost their own Gold Card; a visiting American oral surgeon or a Spanish toxicologist. Spain, that's where Martin and Greta are right now, thinks Kate. Greta and Viv Lingate were surprised that Richard could be grumpy.

My God, thinks Kate, another woman might actually think that Richard's a – her mind skitters away from the concept as if it's a squashed red and hairy thing in the middle of the road but it's still recognisable as a – a sexual being, thinks Kate. My God, no wonder his blazer's crumpled, it's been torn off and thrown on a motel floor before an afternoon of passion. My God, Richard might be grumpy these days because he's spending afternoons in a motel in Greenhithe. Christ, thinks Kate, that could be enough to make anyone grumpy – a motel in Green-hithe.

No, thinks Kate, Richard has every right to be grumpy, he lives under an enormous amount of pressure, he should spend half an hour in a decompression chamber each night before he leaves the hospital.

The display shelves have stopped swooping. There's a black high-heeled shoe just like the one Satan tried to digest but sicked back up on the kitchen mat. She asks to try on a pair, size $9\frac{1}{2}$ B. They do wonderful things to her calf muscles. While the assistant

is wrapping them, Kate sees a pair of Bellinis, red with a brass trim which would be perfect with the gypsy dress, and some red and brown patchwork sandals, both pairs with the exact height of heel that Kate's most comfortable in, about $1\frac{1}{2}$ inches. 'Those,' says Kate. There's a dashing pair of black sports shoes with thick soles and high ankles, and she hasn't had a new pair of slippers for a year. And a pair of soft grey moccasins for round the house. My God, thinks Kate, and I was sorry I didn't help him get that travel money. Why didn't I unfold the invoice, dble $118 pd cash, when I was in a more expensive shoe shop? So she buys a pair of flat-soled Sergio Armanis too. Seven pairs of shoes. Seven.
 That's a lucky number, thinks Kate.

When Kate arrives home she gives Satan a big love, because even though she loathes him she loves him too. He's been a fixture in her life for eight years since they rescued him from the SPCA and she won't be able to bear it if he ever dies. She unpacks the groceries and sends him outside with a new rawhide bone.

Owen has left her a note: Job hunting. Employment-exchanging. Loving you – the Great Mistake.

Kate begins to cry. It isn't fair that Owen thinks he's a mistake. Losing his job has done awful things to his self-confidence. He's being brave and resourceful, but it's always been so hard for him. He's just as clever if not more so than the girls, but Richard expected more of him, so Owen has opted out of conventionally clever things. Kate knows. A mother always knows.

Kate makes a pot of tea and takes it to the sunroom. It overlooks the patio, the terracotta pots and the lemon tree. She puts her feet up on the cane sofa with its plumpy gold and cream cushions, and there's a matching armchair and glass-topped table and there's the latest *Metro* magazine casually arranged on the table with a copy of *Australian House and Garden* so everyone would think she's a woman who has everything *ha ha ha*.

She is still crying, and that's stupid so she blows her nose. Satan lollops over the lawn and puts his paws up on the French doors, stares at her, then flops away. She holds a fresh tissue over her eyes.

Kate has discovered that her husband is having an affair. She is very brave. Noble behaviour is the way to go. Since she is no longer enough for him, she will take herself out of his life. Graciously, elegantly, she tells Richard she is going to a meeting of the Friends of the Mercury Theatre. — That went bust years ago, says Richard. — That's why it needs Friends, she answers gently. — I may be gone some time, says Kate. He doesn't say: when did you become a Friend and how much did that cost me? He grunts into the Letters to the Editor section of the *Blood & Guts Medical Journal*. She stands behind him, breathes a soft kiss on the back of his head where he's still got hair. There is a lump in her throat. She'll never follow his Quickstep again, never know him when he's old and grey. Mind you, he's losing his hair faster than it's losing colour.

She strokes the keys of her beloved Yamaha upright, lowers the lid. Then, for the last time, she leaves the house, the cane sofa, the unread *Metro*, the dishwasher. She has a bottle of — um? — Jacob's Creek with her. It isn't expensive but can be trusted to be potable. Two bottles. Better have a bottle opener too.

She drives through the scented Auckland night to the

Waitakeres — will that be comfortable? — it's usually damp there. No, it's all right, she won't notice the ground conditions for long.

At the end of a deserted road, she parks the Chariot and locks it carefully. She has a blanket with her. She is — how am I dressed, thinks Kate? My new black sports shoes, and a tracksuit, that should do.

She back-pedals for a moment: — Are you dressed for a meeting? asks Richard. — The theatre's been dead for so long, Kate struggles nobly, personfully, to refrain from letting her chest heave with emotion, — that it's casual, she says.

She locks the Chariot, and forces her way into the dew-soaked bush. A morepork calls, as if the solitary night-bird beckons her to a secluded grove where no one will discover her and her pain until the night has done its work. She spreads the blanket on the ground. She un-corks bottle one of Jacob's Creek. Hang on, a wine glass? Right, she's brought one of those hand-painted goblets, they hold heaps.

The morepork calls again: — Moore — poork, chiming Kate onward to oblivion. A hedgehog comes close to snuffle at her hand. She is one with the spirits of the bush, she is a Friend of the Earth, dust to dust and so on, thinks Kate. The wine-warmth eases her, soothes, per-meates her veins, red life-blood, sensual. Oblivion.

— Moore-poork.

Kate sips her cup of tea. Meals on Wheels first, thinks Kate. And I'd better wait till Owen's got a job. And Jessica's got to get through the sixth form. And I haven't worn any of my new shoes yet. And why should Richard get off so lightly?

Because bloody hell, thinks Kate, if he is having an affair, he's bloody not going to get away with all my life insurance.

chapter six

K ate has been sent home by Meals on Wheels.

Mashed potatoes reclining on a doorstep
bedecked with cabbage under an avalanche of gravy.

She will have to do something. Trouble is, she doesn't
know what. When Amelia's distressed she comes to her little
sister and weeps, and is soothed with cups of tea and given good
advice. Kate figures it's Amelia's turn to do the tea and
sympathy.

But by four o'clock Amelia still hasn't answered the phone.
Barry and Amelia don't have an answerphone, they say it's
technological pollution but Kate knows they can't afford one.
Kate has sat at the piano and played her own particular version
of 'Solveig's Lament' then gone to the phone again. Still no
answer. Kate doesn't think it's fair. Not when she needs help.
And Amelia's the obvious person, since she knows about affairs.
For a second, Kate wonders why she's so upset if Richard's
having an affair, because they haven't had that much of a sex life
for a year or two anyway, apart from the nice little burst in
January. But that's normal. Isn't it? At their age? And if Richard
wanted more of a sex life, he'd come to bed earlier. Wouldn't he?

Outside, there's a thump. Owen's bike. She stands in the
hallway, holding the phone. Owen comes past, dressed in his
interview clothes with the pastel shirt and the pastel-flowered

tie – she can't understand why he's such a stick when he goes through so much peanut butter – and climbs the stairs. He shuts his door. It opens again.

'You all right, Mum?'

She wiggles her free hand in a vaudeville flutter: ▆◀ *let's go-oh on with the show-oh!*

Owen disappears again. Kate stabs redial on the phone. She'd like to cry again. But the front door crashes open. Jessica whirlwinds by into the kitchen, littering the hall with her school cardigan, a magazine with a particularly ugly rock star on the cover, and her schoolbag which is plastered in fluorescent stickers that cry out *Save the Whales*. Kate swallows her tears.

'Mrs Ferlin is a load of cat vomit!' Jess bangs open one kitchen cupboard after another. 'How dare she be so rude to the street kids, they have the right to go wherever they like if their own parents don't want them!' She sticks her head through the door, flaps her hands at Kate and disappears again, still shouting. 'Why shouldn't they hang around the school gates, why does Mrs Ferlin have to get so rat-shit? I'll talk to them if I want, how dare that CatVomit snarl at me! I'll complain to the Board of Trustees!' Jessica rushes out of the kitchen with two muesli bars in her hand. 'Mum, she makes me so mad . . . '

Amelia's voice speaks in Kate's ear. 'Umph?' She sounds breathless. 'Kate, I've been filming since 5 am. An ad for cookies. They taped my breasts for more uplift. It's still the dark ages. If it wasn't for the money!'

Kate flicks a hand for Jessica to go away. 'Amelia – are you free tomorrow?' Kate will sleep on it. That's really sensible. And noble. And she can't cry now the kids are home. Jess dashes upstairs and her favourite scrambly guitar tape starts thumping full volume. Owen shouts at her to shut up and turns on his own stereo. 'What?' Kate asks Amelia. 'What?'

'Come in the morning. I've got a pupil at midday, that's all. Kate? Are you all right?'

'We'll need a big pot of tea,' says Kate.

Amelia has had the kettle ready boiled, waiting. 'No,' she says. 'Oh no.' The invoice is on the wooden veneer table in the open plan kitchen-living area, rainbowed by the rays that fall through the crystal hanging in the window.

'So what does this mean?' Kate pushes the invoice towards Amelia. Kate has walked here. She doesn't trust herself to drive. Satan's tied to a tree stump: he can pee on that because it's already dead, or on the concrete fence post. He's exhausted after the long walk but strains at his leash, whimpering because he wants to come and love Amelia.

'Oh,' says Amelia. 'There might be an explanation – ' She passes the invoice back quickly and wipes her hands on her Indian cotton trousers.

'Thank God.' Kate sits back in the old bentwood. Her bones feel peculiar. She doesn't know if they feel light or heavy. But Amelia will settle her down, she's sure.

'What a bastard. My sister. How could he do this to my sister?'

A frown arrives and sits between Kate's eyebrows. 'Hang on, you have affairs. That's why I came. You can explain. You understand. Even right now you want to sleep with – who? The one with the name like a toilet cleanser?'

'Drystan.' Amelia doesn't look very pleased. 'But I haven't. Not yet. Anyway, it's different.'

'Um – because Barry never knows,' says Kate.

Amelia grabs Kate's mug and tops it up. 'It's not just that. There's meaning to it, when I do. I get in touch with myself through all the . . . ' Amelia's mouth starts to go loose and the orange flicker shows for a moment in her eyes. She swallows and makes her mouth go prim. 'Could it be – making Richard get in touch with himself?'

Kate's voice is a mix of wail and growl. 'That's it! That's it exactly! I must have failed Richard! Tell me where I went wrong!'

'Oh, Kate.' Amelia sounds awed now. 'How dare he? You're just the perfect wife. I've always envied how you manage things. I have disastrous muddles with just one child. You've managed three, and Satan, not to mention Richard. How could he! He's never had to worry about a thing at home. You gave up your career just so he could follow his without having to worry about who minds the kids, who takes the car in for an oil and grease, who picks up the dry-clean . . . ' Amelia stops and eyes the invoice.

'What career? I hated being a nurse.'

'Your music,' says Amelia.

'Who cares about that?' Kate thought she was puzzled and confused already, but she's feeling worse and worse. 'I couldn't practise while Richard was studying. We couldn't afford a piano then anyway. I've never even had a part-time job – with three small kids – ' Kate has never regretted that she's put her time into being a wife and mother. She's enjoyed being a mother-help at school and doing her voluntary work. 'Oh God, I didn't do enough! I was a companion to Fish and Bird but not to Richard, is that it? I should have taken self-improvement classes. I should have done Russian after all! Why didn't Richard tell me I wasn't interesting enough!' God, all she's done for him lately is walk Satan. Who has stopped whimpering and is lying on the driveway with his nose on his paws, watching the house as if it contains the epitome of all his desires and will forever be too far away to reach. Kate's eyes burn with tears. 'Do you have affairs because Barry isn't interesting enough? I think Barry's lovely!'

'I'm very worried that you're blaming yourself.' Clearly Amelia will not answer Kate. Her expression is one Kate was frightened of in old family photographs, the jaw-clench of the pioneer women who stocked the country with backbone and determination and with babies who grew up to be cannon fodder for the English to use in World War One. *If that's the case, then let's get on with it*, says the expression. Kate knows she'll be told by her big sister: *Wait till it's over, it will soon be over, it never lasts long for me.* And: *Go on as if nothing has happened.* She doesn't expect Amelia to say: *Go home to Mother,* because Amelia knows affairs aren't all that serious, even though she is upset for Kate. Besides, Mother is seventy-five years old, has Alzheimer's and is in a nursing home in Dunedin. Kate imagines what the matron would say if she arrived on the doorstep with Satan and a suitcase but Amelia snaps her back to the kitchen-living area and the pot of tea.

'Should I tell Barry, I wonder. Would it help if Barry talked to Richard?'

'No!' Not when Richard knows about Amelia's affairs. And Richard despises Barry. Partly because Owen, Alice and Jessica think Barry is superb. Barry's an arborist. He saves native trees. The children used to worship Barry when they were little. 'He's so brave,' they used to say. 'He climbs the tallest trees. He's so little and fat, but he climbs the big tall trees and saves them from the possums!' 'I save lives,' Richard used to say, 'that's pretty good.' 'Oh sure,' the kids would say, 'but you don't climb trees to do it.' Kate has longed to tell this to Amelia, but knows it wouldn't do.

'You must get serious help.' Amelia paces the kitchen, back and forth between the old earthenware flour crock and the sack of organically grown potatoes. 'You need the community of womanhood to help you get through this. You need an en-counter group, Kate.'

'Richard's the one having the encounter.' Kate gives her nose a fierce wipe.

'But it's not your fault. Hold fast to that thought, hon!' Amelia puts an arm round Kate and hugs hard. But just as Kate begins to feel safe, she lets go. 'I know — a hypnotist! To help you realise it's not your fault!'

Amelia's getting under Kate's skin again. 'Perhaps I'll get my tarot read,' says Kate sarcastically.

'I don't like the look of you at all. You have to see a counsellor,' says Amelia. 'I love you dearly and I'll help in any possible way but I can't shepherd you through this. You have an incredibly low self-esteem, and it's no good for me to tell you that you honestly are the most wonderful human being, not when you're reacting so badly to a personal crisis. It has to be said by a professional.' Amelia punctuates with wide, artistic arm gestures. 'Or rather, a professional has to guide you to recognise it for yourself.'

Hang on, I wanted help and guidance from my sister, thinks Kate, but at least she's telling me I'm not to blame . . .

'And once you realise you're not to blame – well, you must be, to some extent,' says Amelia, chewing like the rodent she sometimes is through the barricade she has begun to erect for Kate. Kate feels like wailing and growling again. 'With marriage problems, both people must be blamed to some extent. If blame's the right word. I can't think of the right word. And as you know, affairs don't have to be problems in a marriage at all – not in your case, of course,' she adds quickly. She twists her hands in a knot; her forehead's twisted too. Kate starts to feel worried for Amelia. 'Honey, I'm so upset for you. But I am involved, you see. I'm your sister. And if I'm involved, I can't be objective. God, men are awful – I can't believe he's done this to you. Oh, Kate!' Amelia sinks down on a bentwood and leans her elbows on the table. Tears spray out as if she's been punctured. 'You poor, poor hon!' Amelia cries, all mucusy and wet.

Kate stares. Is Amelia in this world, or another one? She's never seen her so upset, not even when that aluminium window engineer begged her to run away with him to the Falklands. But she'll make herself sick if she cries like this for more than a couple of minutes. Kate pats Amelia's back, rubs it, round and round, and pat pat pat. Then she makes another pot of tea and comforts her sister, pat pat, rub, while it steeps. Poor Amelia, this is terrible. An arm round Amelia's shoulders, an unbleached paper towel pulled from the wooden holder on the bench and offered reassuringly. Pat pat. Rub.

When Amelia's sobs have become occasional hiccups, Kate asks, 'You mean, see a psychologist?' She knows a few of the psychologists and psychiatrists around the hospital and she's learned to tell the difference between them and between what they do. She can't remember what the difference is right now, but there is one. Kate feels dizzy. If she went to see whichever one of them, Richard would find out. There's no way she'll let him do that. He thinks psychology and counselling are wanky liberal New Age bullshit as well as rip-offs money-wise. He thinks only the weakest of the weak need professional help of that kind. And he doesn't think it ever does a scrap of good. Amelia's not being much good, either and that's worrying. It's baffling.

'No, no, a counsellor. *Hic.* There are all sorts. Jungian. Crisis management. Personal *hic* development.' Amelia blows her nose and wipes her eyes.

'How do you know?' Kate is more worried than ever for her sister now.

Amelia blushes. She sits up tall and straight in her bentwood. 'Barry sees one sometimes. His height. He's sensitive about not having much.' She stretches out an arm and lifts the Yellow Pages off the phone table. 'Loo-*hic* under C,' she says.

chapter seven

Kate has chosen a counsellor on the North Shore. This is mainly because she likes to drive over the bridge. She especially likes to drive over when the machine is busy moving the concrete blocks which mark the lanes from one side of the middle lane to the other. It is reliable and powerful, and Kate wishes she could drive it. But the machine is hiding while she drives the Chariot over this morning. Kate keeps thinking about the machine because it stops her being scared. In the morning, the bridge has four lanes of traffic coming over from the Shore and two going over from the city. In the evening it's the other way around. The machine shifts the blocks neatly and forcefully from one lane-marking to the other. Then it hides in a long shed until it has to move all the blocks back again. Oh God, it's one thing to reveal your private life to a sister – Amelia knows that Kate's a nut. But in the next hour . . . Why is she doing this? To Kate, all counsellors have German or Swiss accents:

☛ ve haf vays of making you expose yourself.

As Kate parks the car, there's a cramp in her stomach. Hell, she thinks, that'll wreck my concentration – what concentration? She remembered her feminum perteck-shum, as Jessica and Alice call it, this morning but there's no Panadol in her bag. She's nearly late for the appointment, so she quickly checks what she looks like in the driving mirror. Frightful. Somewhere between shock and deep shock. She tries a smile. Out of practice. She doesn't remember smiling much the last few days.

Kate climbs the steps of the address she has written in her diary, and looks at the row of small brass plates. The plate that will be important to her says: Gordon Fitzgarold & Lyllian Spicer, Counselling & Stress Management

She wonders if they do it like a double act. Ginger Rogers, Fred Astaire. No – she'd been asked if she'd like to see Gordon or Lyllian, and she'd fluffed and ummed and said whoever could do her as soon as possible. Anyway, they'd said Thursday because there'd been a cancellation. She hopes it was a cancellation because someone got better, not because they heaved themselves off the bridge. Inside, a receptionist asks her name. Kate is so apprehensive that all she says is, 'Yes.'

'Ah,' says the receptionist. 'First appointment. Mrs Wild-burn.'

In the counsellor's office there's a blue armchair and a desk with a leather executive's chair, and a big blue sofa. A carafe of water, paper cups. A very big box of tissues, opened, and two unopened on a shelf: Kate doesn't like the look of that. Lyllian comes from behind the desk to shake Kate's hand. She is in her fifties, with extraordinary curved red fingernails. Kate is jealous; her own nails have become bitten rag ends over the last three days.

'We'll just chat,' says Lyllian. 'We'll find out something of your life story, if you don't mind, before we get onto what brings you here.' She wears a long-sleeved silk blouse and a big gold watch. She looks like something out of an American mini-series.

'I won't find a single thing to say,' says Kate.

But she begins. She talks about when she got married, and when she had the twins, and when her father died, and when they realised Mother had Alzheimer's but how Mother's still sharp enough to refuse to leave Dunedin so Kate has to visit two or three times a year. Then she talks about how hard Richard works, and how she tries to keep pressure off him at home but it's become more difficult instead of simpler as she'd thought it would, because the children are young adults now and not so easy to fob off with 'Daddy's busy' so he isn't as well protected any more perhaps, but really isn't it time he took some responsibility for himself? She says how awful the trip to Sydney was, and how it was after that she found the invoice in Richard's blazer, and what the date of the invoice was, and how she'd just assumed they were happy but she's obviously got it terribly wrong, and how can she find out what she's done to make him do this? Kate's mouth aches from all the talking. She stops and looks at her watch. 'My God.' She's talked for an hour and a half.

Lyllian makes a don't-panic gesture. 'I always put aside two hours for a first time. Seems to me, you've spent a lot of years taking care of other people. Emotional care. That's wonderful, but there comes a time when you need some in return.'

'I won't do a poor-little-me thing,' says Kate. 'I want to know where I've gone wrong.'

'You want to save your marriage? You still love him?'

Kate feels her eyebrows move into the puzzled position. 'What a funny question.' That's all she can come up with.

'Tell me, then. Richard. Apart from the invoice, how is it that you're sure he's having an affair? Has his behaviour changed lately? Sydney, you said. Tell me one thing about that, for instance, that was unusual.'

'He didn't pack pyjamas.' At once, she wishes she hadn't mentioned that.

'He does his own packing?'

'Since the time I forgot to put his trousers in. He had to speak at a dinner in Perth wearing a dinner jacket and jeans.' Lyllian's mouth opens slightly, almost crooks into a smile. 'God, he was mad. I've never packed for him again. He didn't have time to buy any extra clothes on that trip,' Kate adds, stammering and annoyed with herself, 'he never has time to shop when he's at a conference.'

'He could have popped in somewhere, just for a pair of PJs,' suggests Lyllian.

'No, I did. But he didn't unwrap them. He said it was so hot he'd sleep in his skants.'

Lyllian lifts her chin and stares into the corner of the room for a moment. Then she looks back at Kate. 'Did he know before you went that the sleeping arrangements had been mixed up?' Kate nods. 'There's nothing wrong with being naked,' says Lyllian. 'But it wasn't usual for him, you say. It seems to me that his was a reaction of anger. Misdirected anger. Could he have thought the muddled arrangements were your fault? Your daughter's?'

'Of course not. If he thought that, he was stupid,' says Kate.

Lyllian's expression doesn't change, but there's something pleased in the air. 'Maybe he is stupid,' says Lyllian.

Surely a counsellor ought not to say – Before the outraged thought is complete, Kate's laughing. She hasn't laughed for days. It is amazing how it shakes her whole body, how her face feels rounded and young, alive. She hadn't known how very bad she'd been feeling until now when she feels better. Blood tingles in her hands, her feet. She sits back in the big blue chair and rocks her head in disbelief at how good it feels, while she laughs and laughs and laughs. The counselling costs $80 an hour: worth it, every cent.

'Now,' says Lyllian. 'If he is having an affair, why should that be your fault?'

Kate stops laughing. She feels another cramp low in her stomach and presses a hand into her belly. She's going to have the worst period she's had in years. 'I've run over time, honestly,' she says. 'I need to buy some Panadol.'

Lyllian opens a desk drawer. 'I'm out of them too,' she says. 'But here's some Ponstan. Seems to me this might be what you need.'

'Some what?' Kate reads the packet – the woman on it has a floating head – and pushes it back to Lyllian. 'I'd better not, it hasn't been prescribed.'

'Heavens, you buy it over the counter. Any chemist. I swear by it, not that I need it often these days. The benefits of menopause.' Lyllian pops two capsules from the card and hands them across. 'You'll feel better in half an hour. Guarantee.'

Kate remembers. **I was going to do something about that.** Month after month.

And all you need is your Friendly Local Chemist?

Lyllian pours water into a paper cup and waits while Kate swallows. 'Kate, if Richard thinks it is your fault, it's up to him to tell you so, and tell you why. You don't need to take on any blame unless you know why. You shouldn't have to manage this all by yourself. You can confront him with it, you know.' Lyllian opens a red-covered appointment book and asks when Kate can come again. Kate eyes the box of tissues: she hasn't had to use one. She's not sure if she's pleased by that or not.

Ray Oxford, Kate's Friendly Local Chemist, smiles broadly. 'Mrs Wildburn. And what can I do for you?' He always smiles when he sees Kate. He likes to ask how Dr Wildburn is these days. It lets the other customers know that the chemist knows the doctor and his wife. They usually shuffle. They smile too. Kate always thinks it's weird. It's Mr Wildburn anyway because Richard is a surgeon, but if Ray Oxford said Mr, the customers wouldn't be impressed.

'Some Ponstan, please,' says Kate. There's a lurch of dismay inside when Ray Oxford reaches without looking to a shelf and takes a packet down. $7.90. 'How long has it been available?' asks Kate.

'Months? Years? I'd have to check. Ask your husband, he should know. Something else?' asks the Friendly Local Chemist.

She would like to ask what's the most lethal substance she can buy across the counter. And how much of it can she buy at one time. But she gives a Satisfied Customer Smile and leaves the shop.

Not poisoning, she thinks. Lyllian suggested confrontation. Something within Kate objects. Confrontation would be far too easy. Richard wouldn't suffer long, with confrontation. Besides, she feels she's missing something in this whole situation – and then she realises her cramps have gone. Less than half an hour, as Lyllian guaranteed, and Kate is no longer having the worst period she's had for years.

Head held high, she stands outside the Friendly Chemist's and adopts the jaw-clench bequeathed by pioneer generations. Richard's whirlwind? His little fling? His stalking round with no pyjamas, as his gesture of defiance? The one that said: **Well! Someone thinks I'm sexy, anyhow!**

Kate feels surprisingly calm. I'm at the eye of the storm, she thinks. You can do a lot of planning, at the eye of the storm.

chapter eight

D o you need this for anything?' Kate hands Richard the invoice. 'Tax purposes?'

A strangled noise lodges in his throat. He runs a finger inside his collar and looks away. His head's gone mottled. 'Jeffries,' he says. 'Lost his credit card. I lent him a couple of hundred.' He crumples the invoice. Kate holds out her hand – Kate the Domestic Waste Engineer – and automatically Richard drops the ball of paper into it. He tries to grab it again but she's already walking towards the wastepaper basket as if to use it.

Jeffries like hell, thinks Kate. Jeffries always stays with Greta and Martin when he's in town. Jeffries is a pig and Richard hates him. He wouldn't lend him a broken bean.

She has looked up the latest *AA Accommodation Guide*:

****+ **Glade Motor Inn** 15 Tui Gve, Greenhithe. 10 units sleep 2–5. Kitchen. el range. Microwave. (Some units auto dishwasher.) Brm: double or twin beds. Ph. TV. Vid. Heated swimming pool. Private spa pool. Tariff: $101–118.

He didn't even take one of the cheaper units. He had an automatic dishwasher for his afternoon of sin.

Kate has taken up her bow of burning gold, her arrows of resolve. She has put on the breast plate of righteousness. She wears the buskins of retribution, not to mention the ruthless spurs of vengeance. She is the Warrior Queen, and she will ride the storm.

2

Smorgasbörd

[EXPERIENCE]

chapter nine

Strategy. The Warrior Queen has planned to have a planning session, after doing the laundry and wiping the keys of the Yamaha upright and writing a letter to Mother which the dear old pet won't remember even if she reads it but at least it helps Kate feel she's doing her duty.

Strategy! What does Kate know about objectives and deployment? She has a go at planning dinner parties, family holidays and expeditions to Big Fresh. She can more or less plan what to leave for the family in the pantry and freezer when she goes to Dunedin. But a battle campaign? All she can think is how hard it would be to explain to the car dealers in Manukau Road why she absolutely has to have scythes fitted to the front wheels of the Mitsubishi Chariot.

I'm still missing something important, she thinks. I need another brain in on this, a Battle-Maid. Amelia's useless: she finds the whole business too upsetting. Besides, Amelia's morals are confusing – how can she have one attitude towards her own affairs and a thoroughly different one to Richard's? Poor Kate, poor Barry, thinks Kate. Mind you, she tells herself, pouring her fourth cup of coffee for the morning, Drystan can't help but look more appealing than the Wobbly Man, no matter how brave Barry is at shinning up a rimu. She pictures the choreography of her sister and the aerobics instructor in aerobic contortions while Barry reels around them waving boughs from native saplings in an aerobically symbolic representation of delayed revenge. That's what Kate is doing too: delaying. Now Libby'd be a suitable recruit . . .

A *click*! outside tells her the postie's put some mail in the box. Satan and Kate run out to see. There's some junk mail, a bill and a letter from Alice.

Satan smells Alice on the letter. Kate sniffs it too: a whiff of her beautiful brown-haired daughter. She lets Satan chew the envelope while she takes her coffee to the sunroom. She wants to feast on the five closely written pages, savour them like hot, salty chips. Alice is having a terrific time. Christchurch is so quaint, old-fashioned, everything makes her laugh. The job's awful though, waitressing for up-themselves yuppies with more money than manners; they make her yech and puke. The course is hard too. Teeline makes her sweat – that's Shorthand, she explains. Her first big assignment isn't due till after Easter, but Alice thinks she's doing all right so far. She misses home more than she thought. Can she come up for Easter? She misses Kate like crazy. She misses Jessica, and Owen, and Satan. Oh – Dad too.

Kate enjoys the tears that fill her eyes and tickle her nose. It's amazing, being a mother. Amazing how you love each child the best, how the love is so uncomplicated though it's all-encompassing, deep and wide, as important as breathing, as necessary as your heartblood.

The Warrior Queen has been distracted. This, thinks Kate, is reprehensible in a Commander in Chief. She sits up straight. Think! Satan appears, a shred of envelope hanging from his lower lip. He tries to bite the bill too. Kate pushes him out the French doors. The bill is for insurance. She hasn't taken much notice of things financial lately. Richard's always too busy to notice things financial. **Work comes first**, and he rucks out another blood, sweat and tears agenda. Ha bloody ha. What's first, these days, is spending money on sporting equipment and court time for squash, his euphemism for motel rooms maybe.

It's nearly three weeks till the bank statement's due. It will be at the limit of the overdraft. There'll be the cheque for seven pairs of shoes: $673 was very good, thinks Kate It could have been far worse – if the winter stock had been in, I'd have bought a pair of knee-high leather boots as well. But she'll pay the insurance right away. It's Richard's life insurance.

The phone rings, distracting her again. I don't want to speak to Amelia, she thinks. But it's Mrs Ferlin, from the college.

'How is Jessica?' asks Mrs Ferlin.

'Fine,' says Kate.

'It's a pity she's missed so much school.' The teacher's voice is like cream sauce over witloof. Kate winces. Witloof's the most bitter vegetable she's ever tasted and she can't figure out why people pretend it's delicious.

'She caught up quickly after that week in Sydney,' says Kate. The Warrior Queen is ready to become an Avenging Angel. Two AA tasks: One: protect Jessica, whom she loves the best of all her children, from Mrs Ferlin; Two: shred Jessica into flakes no bigger than wheatgerm if she's been skipping classes. She adopts her own witloof and cream sauce combination. 'Jessica's fine. I appreciate your concern.' She sees Satan tear across the lawn towards the gate. He may be about to terrify a pair of Seventh Day Adventists so Kate puts the phone down.

It's Owen. He comes in, hand wound into Satan's collar. Even though it's still summer, even though he's been riding his bike each day looking for work, he is pale. Though he always looks smart. When Owen wears decorated bicycle clips on his fashionable baggies, Richard makes coughing noises and gives glances of appeal to the ceiling. But Kate thinks Owen always looks hip-cool, even when he seems beaten, like right now.

'No luck?' Kate's heart breaks: she loves him the best of all her children.

'Three places said I've got a good record but they want someone older with more experience. Three places said they want someone younger so they won't have to pay as much. The last place can't afford anyone after all. I've had enough for today.' Owen kneels and rubs his head on Satan's. 'At least you don't mind me staying here.'

Kate's heart breaks again. 'Let's go somewhere special. You and me. Lunch at a trendy pub and we'll have wine.' The overdraft can go to hell.

But Owen keeps his head resting on Satan. 'I'll grab a sandwich. Got some phone calls to make.' He disappears into the kitchen. Kate wants to yell after him not to leave a mess, she's just done the floor, and please remember to wipe the bench. But she doesn't. There are other ways to make your family do their bit to keep things clean – she'll find them one day.

She's beginning to feel claustrophobic. Yes, high time she saw Libby, her very best friend in all the world. She dials, and leaves a message on the answerphone: *Help help and rescue, lunch in Parnell, Monday please.*

She doesn't need to say who it is. Libby will know.

Monday morning. Kate doesn't tell Richard she's having lunch with Libby. She suspects he's suspicious of her intelligent women friends, though he doesn't mind her meeting the other doctors' wives occasionally. Kate has never been able to fathom, actually, why Libby is her best friend and has been for over fifteen years. Libby is articulate, effervescent, so startlingly clever she makes Kate feel like a stuffed pigeon.

Because it's Libby, and because it's Parnell, Kate takes a long time deciding what to wear. Pink cotton trousers, a black belt with a cougarhead buckle. A black designer T-shirt, tucked in. Pearl and gold dangly earrings – so tacky they're irresistible. She stands in front of the mirror and makes a face. Super, darling. But next to Libby she'll look as if she shops at the Salvation Army.

Last thing before she leaves, she puts away yesterday's laundry. That means dumping Owen's and Jessica's on the floor outside their bedroom doors as usual. At least they put their own dirty clothes down to be washed. Richard doesn't, though he yells at the kids if they're untidy. Once she left his things un-picked-up for a full week but did he notice? When she asked him about it, he said, 'What do I pay you for, Kate?' and quickstepped her round the bedroom so fast they tumbled onto the bed, and made her giggle so much she thought she'd let it ride.

In the main bedroom, she puts her own clothes into their drawers, hangs up her blouses and so on. Then she puts Richard's clothes away. She puts the socks in his T-shirt drawer, and his weekend T-shirts in the underwear drawer. His skants she puts in the lowest drawer where he keeps his winter sweaters. The freshly ironed shirts she puts at the far end of his closet, behind his dinner suit and Swanndri, the things he only uses once or twice a year. There'll be a dreadful fuss tomorrow. As she swings out of the room, she catches another glimpse of herself in the mirror. Her eyes are glittering. Perfect for Parnell after all.

They meet at Quentin St John's. They always do: they pretend they've met by accident. Initially, the shop assistant — in this store, they're dressed more like madams — ignores them. The first to arrive begins to look carefully at all the satin ballgowns, the silks and taffetas, the feathers and embroidery, and the other one pretends to notice her friend just because she's passing. This time, Libby is already there when Kate comes down the road. She hopes she can play the game as well as usual, so takes a good long breath before she steps in. '*Delilah?* 'Lilah, it's *you!*' says Kate as she enters, arms spread wide.

'*Guinevere!*' cries Libby. They fall upon each other's necks and hug.

'How was South *America*?' they say. 'Was lunch with the *Cabinet* all right, then?' And: 'I saw your mention in *Time*, darling, how splendid!' The madam begins to hover at this point. 'Are you buying, darling?' asks Kate. 'What does one *wear*, to a *third wedding*?' asks Libby. 'Your *own*?' asks Kate. 'My *first husband's*,' says Libby. They decide nothing here's quite suitable, and play the same game in another lavish-your-dollars boutique further up the road. 'This would be *darling*,' says Kate, drawing a red and black almost-flamenco gown from one of the racks. It has ruffles and a trailing skirt. It has a low-cut bodice and only one sleeve: the other shoulder's bare. It would be a dangerous dress to wear; you'd have to use Elastoplast or glue to keep it up. 'Does it come with its own tube of adhesive?' asks Kate. It has a four-figure price tag.

'Number Three will be wearing something cheaper, I expect. I don't want to show them up too much,' says Libby. They smile thank you to the assistant and saunter out. Over the intersection, they clutch each other and giggle, then continue up the road to find a place to eat. Libby isn't dressed as magnificently as usual. She does have a wonderful belt made of chased brass tiles. Otherwise, she's very conservative in trousers and neat scoop-necked blouse. Kate wonders why.

'How's Richard's battle for the funds?' asks Libby as they pass a horrifyingly expensive kitchenware boutique.

'Blow that. I've got other fish to fry. You'll hear,' says Kate. 'What are you doing dressed like that?'

'Frying other fish. New client. Two-storey house, just up the road a bit.' Libby waves, indicating it's up the road and round the corner and way down the other road. 'A fabulously eccentric old woman with an even more eccentric brother – he lives next door. I'm working on him for a contract, too. He hasn't bitten but I'll get him in the end. I'm doing her all

Renaissance. Would you believe it? Me! Two years ago I had a marriage settlement and no future. And now! But we'll hear about your fish first.'

The place with the parrot's always nice. They choose a table outside and order salads. *Ah-lo! Ah-lo!* says the parrot.

'Glass of wine?' asks Libby.

'Bottle,' says Kate.

Libby's mouth makes an ooo shape and she says, 'My treat.' When they're sipping the first glass of chardonnay, Libby says, 'Well, then?'

'Guess,' says Kate.

Libby is still not really sure if Kate's in trouble, for she wears a half-smile. 'Jessica's anorexic?' Jess is notorious for the amount of fish and chips she can eat at one sitting. Kate shakes her head. 'Alice has become an anti-vivisectionist and uses a loudspeaker on those amazing marches?' Alice is famous for being an observer and reporter, not a participant. Kate shakes her head. 'Owen's pregnant? Oh God, Kate, you're not pregnant!'

Kate digs through her bag for the invoice. It's well-thumbed by now but no longer crumpled. Kate has ironed it.

'Greenhithe?' Libby picks up the invoice, and puts it down again. 'When I was little, we used to visit a scary old woman out there. She lived in a cottage covered in wisteria. There was a well and frogs and great big huhu bugs . . . '

'Now it's the outskirts of the urban jungle, and I found that in Richard's pocket.' Kate finishes her first glass of wine.

Libby stares at Kate before peering at the invoice more closely. Then she drains her own glass. At last, she says: 'Who is it?'

'Who's what?' asks Kate.

'The other woman. Who is she?' Libby sloshes out more wine for them both.

There is a pause, then the other tables begin the same swooping dance as the shelves in the shoe shop when Kate first found the piece of paper. The parrot bobs like a yo-yo, up and down and round. The sunshine's very spangly, dotted with black patches. 'She?' says Kate. 'Of course. If he — if he's having an affair — ' The edge of the table is swinging up to hit her.

'It's with another woman,' says Libby. 'Quick, put your head between your knees.'

Next thing Kate knows, the waitress and the chef are beside the table fanning her with menus. There's a jumble of voices, high-pitched questions. Libby tries to make her sip a glass of water. Kate pushes it away. She sits up, knees together, both hands on the table, and takes a deep breath. *Slow, slow, quick, quick, slow.* Her breathing's doing a foxtrot. She's all right now. She's just proved that she's even more stupid than she'd thought so now she's hopping mad. But Libby's brilliant. She's found the missing piece. She will be an excellent Deputy in the coming Campaign.

'I know just how you feel.' Libby stabs a fork into her shrimp-laden avocado.

'Geoff wasn't unfaithful, was he? I know you wondered, but — ' Kate puts a spoon into her own pile of shrimp then takes it out again. Libby's been divorced for three years. She's living with an architect named Kennedy Jonah now. That's how Libby got into interiors. It's always who you know, it's never what you know. Geoff was a divorce lawyer who spent so much time on his clients' separation agreements that he didn't know his own was being drawn up by another lawyer in the suite on the floor below.

'Geoff? Affairs? I never knew for sure — ' Libby points her chin upwards and twiddles her wine glass. She's blasé now, but Kate remembers Libby curled in a foetal ball on Kate's cane sofa, face so swollen with anguish she looked like a five-year-old, helpless and inconsolable.

'I want to work out what to do,' says Kate. She puts a shrimp on her tongue. It's OK. Her taste buds aren't working as well as usual: it's Richard's fault and it's a crying shame.

'Are you going to leave him?'

Kate reaches for her wine. But her hand shakes so she puts it in her lap and holds it tightly with the other one. *Ah-lo! Ah-lo!* squawks the parrot.

'Because if you are, there are things you must organise. I've been through it, love, I know.'

'Slow down, Lib. Slow down.'

'Have you got your own cheque account? Separate credit card?' Libby bites efficiently into her garlic bread. 'We'll go to a bank after lunch and get you started.' Her head tilts to one side. She and the parrot are looking at Kate in exactly the same way. Bright blue eyes, and yellow-brown eyes. 'You don't still love Richard, do you? After twenty years?' Libby has put incredulity into her blue eyes, and scepticism on her bright red mouth.

That's what Lyllian Spicer asked. I'd better think about it, Kate says to herself. She takes her chardonnay in both hands. What, after all, is love?

Walking to Richard's flat following your late shift on geriatrics, with Richard who's studying for fifth year. Snow starting to fall, your nose is running and your feet wet through, but Richard's feeling randy so even though you're near a street light he tries to put his hand inside your duffel coat and you nearly slip on a muddy patch. You're cold, exhausted, but you're laughing and wanting him so much.

Applause from the sides of the Union Hall, from the crowds of students drunken-happy under the streamers and glitter ball, as you and Richard realise everyone else has stopped dancing and they're watching you spin out of his arms and back again, a dip, a flourish, everyone clapping and cheering.

Richard telling people you're the one to ask about music, because you studied piano for eleven years and should have gone further, but your parents said you had to have a career first: nursing, which you never finished because you got pregnant. Richard saying: their short-sightedness worked to my advantage though, because otherwise I might never have met you.

Lying under Richard, holding his shoulders, sweet bare flesh, feeling the pressure inside build and build in an enormously exciting way, and Richard collapsing just as you're sure that at last you'll find out what the secret is, the secret everyone else knows.

Waiting for Richard to come home after he's been on duty all weekend and it's gone 8.30 Monday night. The twins haven't seen him since Friday morning and they're cranky, it's hours past their bedtime. And you're eight months pregnant again, and when he does get home you're going to scream, can't he even have the courtesy to give you a phone call if he's going to be so late! And when he does get home his skin is papery with tiredness and all you do is smile because you're so relieved he hasn't had an accident on that damn three-way intersection.

Asking Richard what he thinks of minimalist music, and knowing you'll have a proper conversation for the first time in years, a conversation where you'll both learn more about the other one, not just a chat about the price of school uniforms, and the way the mortgage never gets less before Richard has his nightly rail about what went wrong in surgery committee today. And Richard sputtering: Minimalist! Tuneless rubbish, don't tell me you're listening to that crap. And him slamming the table with his open hand, thump! and beginning to talk about what went wrong at work today. And you feeling that you've been left out on a ridge somewhere and it's too dark to see the way down.

Hearing: S'this something you want? And unfolding the rectangle of paper: Greenhithe. $118 inc. GST.

'Love?' says Kate. Why, otherwise, would she be so angry, so determined to do – something. Just as Libby loved and maybe still loves Geoff, even three years and a new love later. Of course she loves Richard, it's like a wart, once you have it you can't do much about it.

She has another sip of wine. Her hand's still shaking. But the shaking has become a stronger kind. There's toughness in it. It's tough like energy, or fierceness. With a hot jolt under her ribs, she realises why she's shaking. With Warrior Queenliness, of course.

'To hell with love,' says Kate, 'I've done all that. If there's another woman in the case, it's revenge I'm after now.'

Libby has been watching her. She sees Libby has clenched one hand into a fist. She bangs it down. The centre vase of pansies wobbles. Libby lifts her glass. 'Revenge,' she says. 'Aha!'

chapter ten

The Battle Plan: preparations:
1: know the enemy
the enemy: 1.1: she

'She,' says Libby, over coffee. 'We need to find out who it is. I'm assuming it's one woman, not several. And I don't think Richard's got a secret gay side to him. Has he?'

A delightful image blossoms in Kate's mind: Richard clad like a campy game show host in a sequinned body suit. 'He's into sporting mateship, that's all,' she manages before she splutters her espresso on the table. It's like when she talked to Lyllian. The laughter feels so good, even if it is closer to hysterical this time.

Libby pats Kate's arm. 'So, any idea who she is?' Kate lifts her shoulders. 'Hmmm . . .' Libby taps her fingers on the table. 'Would an impressionable young nurse be impressed by Richard?'

'No. He's as grumpy at work as he is at home.'

'She might be impressed by how much he earns.'

'Well – the main thing about a surgeon's salary is that though it's high, it isn't that high. I mean, it hasn't been very much until the last seven years or so. And it's not as high as the academics get. He's too busy to go into private practice, that's where the money would be. The biggest thing we've been able to do on Richard's salary is get a huge overdraft. And a bigger mortgage. He's really annoyed we still can't buy a boat.'

'A *what*?' Libby's face screws up. She and Geoff, with Kate and Richard, went sailing once. Mirror-calm harbour. Richard vomited all the way.

'There are those seasick patches now. Don't you stick them behind your ear? Richard longs to have what everyone else has. He'll have a boat one day if it kills him.'

'There's your answer,' mutters Libby. 'Anyway, a nurse. If she's a wee nursie bimbo with blonde hair and big eyes and a teensy waist, Kate, you've got no chance.'

'Thanks,' says Kate. 'Women can be such bitches, had you noticed?'

'I'm being realistic.' Libby signals the waitress for more coffee.

'I was a nurse too, remember.'

'You were far too intelligent for that,' says Lib.

'Most nurses are,' says Kate, 'that's why it's probably not a nurse.'

'So, is it one of your friends – an unintelligent one? Someone he's met through work?'

Kate shrugs again. But that blonde-haired drug rep had a very old-fashioned line in PR. Young enough to be a daughter. Richard couldn't be that crass. But oh my God, what about a medical student – no, Kate reassures herself, that only happens with literature professors and their students. She hopes.

'Think!' Libby orders. 'You say his behaviour's changed. Over the last three months, you said. He's even more grumpy, and he's taken up squash. When was the first time he was different? The very first.'

It's late March now. Three months ago was Christmas. Christmas was fine. New Year? They went to a party given by a couple who are a cardiologist and a pharmacologist. Richard made jokes about the pharmacological quality of the punch. Tom and Viv were there. The Osbenes – Brenda Osbene's beautiful. Jeffries and his wife were up from Hamilton. A long-legged stockbrokeress. An archaeology researcher with antique bracelets. An importer with a pert little bust. When the clock struck, everyone kissed everyone else whether they knew them or not. Kate's read in books how a simple little kiss can electrify a person's sexual consciousness. Oh yeah? It's never happened to her. Could someone have given Richard an electric kiss, at a drunken New Year party?

'He was in an incredibly good mood just after New Year,' says Kate. 'Then he went grumpy. I can't be more helpful than that.'

'Do you think it's only one other woman?' Libby sounds cautious.

Kate's growing annoyed. 'For all I know, it could be you.' Libby lets out a shout of disbelief that makes the parrot flutter on its perch. 'Honestly, Lib, I'm surprised he's found the energy and spare time for one other woman. He'd never cope with two.'

the enemy: 1.2: he

'Now why has he suddenly gone off the rails,' says Libby. 'I assume this is the first time. Or is it just the first you've found out about?'

'Lunch with you was not a good idea,' says Kate.

'OK, he's been too busy for an affair before now. Maybe he's wanted to, though, if he thinks everyone else does. Maybe this time the other woman is just extremely pushy, very determined. Do you know anyone who's pushy and determined?'

'You,' says Kate. Libby purses her lips but Kate doesn't want to help. She knows she's being contradictory. She'll be as contradictory as she pleases.

Libby sighs. 'Every woman becomes pushy and determined when she wants a man,' she says. 'You're right, they can be bitches.' Lib sighs again. 'Why? Why would he do it? An affair gives you a tremendous buzz,' she muses. 'Especially when you're over forty.'

'Remind me. Did you leave Geoff before or after you met Kennedy?' asks Kate.

Libby slides a sideways look at Kate, who slides one back. 'How's your sex life?' asks Libby. 'Treat my question in a clinical light and remember, you did want my advice.'

'Once or twice a week,' says Kate. 'That's normal.'

'Normal,' Libby agrees, 'but is it fun? What if someone's made Richard feel like a young buck again? What if he's feeling all-powerful again, the way men do when they're twenty?'

'What if he's met someone who's his idea of the ideal woman?' Kate is feeling vengeful again. 'What if he's met someone like his mother!'

'Attagirl,' says Libby. 'Now you're hot.'

The Battle Plan: preparations:
2: check the terrain
the terrain: 2.1: Richard

'Take notice of him when he comes in at night,' says Libby.

'He gets a kiss hullo,' says Kate.

'I didn't say kiss him, I said take notice. Are his clothes crumpled? If so, have they been lying on a motel floor?'

Kate has another sidetrack thought. 'You'd hope so, wouldn't you? I mean, if you were having an affair and the man took time to hang his clothes up, wouldn't you be peeved?'

'Concentrate!' says Libby. 'Is he more tired than usual after work?'

'Sometimes he plays squash,' says Kate.

'Check his sports bag. Are the clothes wet? Do they smell? Of sweat? Does he smell? Is it aftershave or Opium?'

'If it's Opium it might be mine,' says Kate. 'No, sometimes I wear Poison and I don't get into his sports bag much.'

Libby flashes a you're-so-tiresome look at Kate. 'And what about his face? Are his lips red and well used? Tip of his nose all shiny? Little scratch marks on his back?'

'You know a lot about it.'

'Believe me,' Libby says.

the terrain: 2.2: other women

'When you're out, keep an eye on him. See who he talks to. See who he avoids. See who keeps glancing at him. See who doesn't glance his way. Remember who he talks about when you're driving home. Remember who he doesn't talk about. If someone phones your home, ask their name. If it's a woman, say he's late tonight and you don't know why. Say that even if you do know why. Even if he is home, tell her he's out and you don't know why. If it's her, she'll get highly pissed-off. Pissed off with him. You'll be able to tell if it's her.'

the terrain: 2.3: Kate

'Take a good look at yourself. What are your strengths? Looks, I'd say,' says Libby. 'And your deep and secret capacity for subversion. Work on it.'

'Um . . . ' says Kate.

'Take another look at yourself, and figure out what you can do that will make him sit up. Start looking for a job.'

'What the hell could I do!'

'Pity you're too old for cabaret.' Libby eyes Kate up and down. 'With your piano, and your looks, you could be stunning.'

'You are dreaming,' says Kate. But wouldn't that annoy Richard to the utmost? Wouldn't it be exciting, to have permission for open flamboyance . . . Kate feels a huge bubble in her chest, impossible dream, a longing for adventure.

'And you've got a brain for maths.' Libby flutters her fingers to show how hard she's thinking about this. 'Something will occur to me. But you must be serious about looking for work. That'll shock him out of his complacency. That'll make him look at you with fresh eyes.'

The Battle Plan: preparations:
3: know your alternatives
the alternatives: 3.1: divorce

'Don't do it,' says Libby.

'You did,' says Kate.

'So?' asks Libby.

'So why did you leave Geoff?'

'I got desperate. You saw me. I couldn't see an alternative. But think before you do it. Don't, if you can help it,' repeats Libby. 'It's tough out here. There's not a Kennedy under every tree.' Kate puts her chin into the exasperated position. Libby looks exasperated too. 'It should be obvious, Kate. When you leave a prat, no matter what you gain, you could lose just as much. It worries me, you might not be able to handle it, Kate.'

She did, why shouldn't I? thinks Kate. Is Libby being selfish? Is there something wonderful in the unmarried world that she doesn't want me to know about? Is sauce for one goose not sauce for another goose, too? But no, that's real doubt in Libby's face.

'You think I'm a wimp!' says Kate.

'All right, then, do,' says Libby. 'Do get a divorce.'

'No,' says Kate.

the alternatives: 3.2: fight

'Fight as dirty as you can,' advises Libby. 'All's fair. Possession's nine points of the law, and Richard's yours until you decide not to have him any more. There are various ways to fight, and we'll know how once you've studied the terrain more thoroughly. Hurt him in the pocket. Don't ever destroy his pride – no matter how tough men pretend to be, they're tender blooms, remember. Pride's worth more than his balls, to a man. But you can hurt him in the pocket, mortal wounds.'

the alternatives: 3.3: faithfulness

'The cruellest revenge,' says Libby, 'might be to stay faithful. As long as you let him know.'

the alternatives: 3.4: another man

'On the other hand,' says Libby, 'why should he have all the fun?'

The other tables at the parrot place have filled up. One or two customers have been glancing at Kate and Libby: Kate hopes they haven't overheard. The waitress brings the account on a bread and butter plate. 'I said I'd get the wine,' Libby reminds Kate and hands her the bill. 'Here.'

Kate has a quick look. 'Fifteen twenty-five for me, thirty-nine twenty for you.' They leave enough notes on the plate and pick up their bags. Her legs feel wobbly. She wants to go home and collapse.

As Kate and Libby move down from the patio, someone reaches out from a table near the steps.

'Kate?' He stands up. After a second she recalls the moustache. Helco. Marketing manager. John something? He was nice about Owen, at that dinner. 'How nice to see you, Kate.' He has a hand out again, and she takes it.

'You recognised me,' she says, foolishly.

'You're unmistakable.' He grins.

'How's the rat race?' she asks, then thinks, oops, he might think that's a put-down.

But mischief sparks in his eyes. 'No matter how I scurry — splat! Dead end.'

'Still safer than topdressing.' Phew. She's got that right.

His eyebrow does a jiggle which means not-necessarily-safer-believe-you-me. 'When you're round this way again, pop in,' says John: *pop een*, in his Australian twang. The Helco head office must be somewhere near. 'I'll show you round the products.' He winks and turns his mouth down, deprecating the salesman attitude, so that she has to laugh.

She moves out to the street, Libby behind her. The parrot shouts: *Ah-lo. Ah-lo.*

'See?' says Libby. 'It would be easy.'

chapter eleven

Kate feels much more balanced. So much better that when Richard comes out of his morning shower and can't find fresh underwear, she is very cool.

'Things aren't in the right place!'

'There is a right place, for everything, isn't there?' Kate wears her matter-of-fact mother voice.

'Yes.' Richard wears his aggrieved little boy one.

'People should remember that. People shouldn't put anything in the wrong place.' Kate gives him an I-know-what-you've-been-up-to look, which makes him put on an I-don't-know-what-you're-on-about one and bend down quickly and pull out his sportswear drawer. The tips of his ears have gone purplish.

'Hell of a day lined up,' he says loudly. 'Papers club, liver clinic. Don't know why the others on the team can't pull their weight, I see twice as many patients as anyone. When I'll find the time for research, God knows. And those bloody academics say they're the ones who ought to yelp . . . '

She speaks the last line along with him: everyone in the household has known it by heart for years: '. . . the curs, the hounds, slack bastards.'

Hiding her smile as if it is a knife, aware of the compression of Richard's neck and shoulders, the mottle of The Barometer, Kate wraps her dressing gown tightly about her.

In the kitchen, Owen is dressed already and peering in the fridge. Satan's looking too. She takes a packet of doggy bites, shakes some into a bowl then puts the bowl outside. It is Satan's turn to look aggrieved. He thinks indoors is the right place for his bowl of doggy bites.

Owen is still staring into the fridge, pushing his black hair off his forehead, looking worried.

'Muesli?' suggests Kate. 'Yoghurt? There's some muffins. Muffins and marmalade, used to be your favourite.'

He pushes the door to and fills the electric jug. 'Can't think yet. Half asleep.' He sits on the high stool and watches her eat a bowl of muesli. He makes a pot of tea, pours himself a cup, pulls his hair down again into the trendy twist between his eyes. He dabs a finger on the side of Kate's plate, takes a flake of toasted oatmeal.

'What big knuckles you have, grandmama,' says Kate. Owen gives a lop-sided grin. Richard comes in and Owen hops off the stool.

'The Great Mistake. Found a job yet?' Richard looks into the toaster, which is empty, and then at Kate.

'Not overnight, since you last asked.' Owen wears a quiet voice, much quieter than he used to have.

'Dressed for job-hunting, are we.' Richard eyes Owen's blue baggies and the pastel-flowered tie. Owen leaves the room, his tea half-drunk.

Richard looks at the clock. 'Are we out of bread.' His shoulders grow chunkier and thicker, his scalp spottier with disbelief that things are not going as they should this morning.

'Fridge,' says Kate.

He does a neat set of steps that Kate would like to set to music: one towards the fridge, two to the toaster (to check she really hasn't begun to make his toast, that she isn't just teasing), one back towards the fridge, then a sideways hop to the fruit bowl to grab a banana. Still light on his feet, is Richard, could still score a try on the rugby field if the other team were full of idiots running the wrong way.

He drops the peel on the bench and jangles his keys in his trouser pocket. 'Busy day. Seeing the board about my funds. Late home – I've booked a court for six-thirty.'

Kate lifts both hands to his face and kisses him. She'd really like to bite his nose off: she'd like a medal for being so cool. 'Don't tire yourself. Take care.'

She dumps the banana skin in the rubbish bin, in its right place, then nips back to the bedroom to see if he's really taken his sports gear. Yes. She hears Jessica in the shower – she'll be late if she's not careful, and Mrs Cat Vomit will be after her again.

Kate throws her dressing gown and nightie on the bed, and pulls on a pair of trackpants and a T-shirt for Satan's walkies.

As she's opening the front door, Jessica comes running, wrapped in a towel. 'Mum, c'n I have some money? I need some stuff – ' She pushes her wet hair out of her eyes. 'Stuff for school.'

Kate takes twenty dollars from her wallet. Jess looks awkward, so Kate gives her twenty more. 'Go easy. We've still got some Sydney goodies to pay off.'

'Thanks, Keeper of the Family Purse!' Jessica's gone, leaving a trail of drips.

'Your school skirt's in the laundry! I pressed it last night. I do remember telling you to do it,' Kate calls. There's a muffled reply, and the sound of Jessica running up the stairs.

Kate takes her wallet with her. The Friendly Local Chemist will be open soon. Now or never, thinks Kate.

Satan knows the way to Melville Park. He's excited, just like every morning. Kate's excited too, but it's a scary excitement, not like every morning. She keeps looking at her watch. Satan has his pee and several other pees. By the time he's sniffed all the lamp-posts and bushes and street signs that he sniffs every morning and decided that the world is AOK, it's after nine. Kate walks him towards the main road. It isn't fair, to use Ray Oxford for this. Not fair to Richard, that is. So what? I have responsibilities, thinks Kate. To myself, thinks Kate. This will be a new experience, thinks Kate, and:

what's the use of experience if you don't enjoy it?

She ties Satan up outside, flexes her hands and takes a steadying breath. Two other customers. One waiting for a prescription, the other testing the *not tested on animals* range of cosmetics. Ray Oxford in his crisp white chemist-coat steps in front of his assistant in her crisp white chemist-coat and rubs his hands together.

'Mrs Wildburn,' says Ray Oxford. 'And how is Dr Wildburn?'

'Condoms,' says Kate.

The assistant's face and Ray Oxford's face don't change expression. Not exactly. The other customers don't stop what they're doing. Not exactly.

'What range have you got?' asks Kate.

Ray Oxford bends one arm at the elbow and points sideways, like a marionette. Of course Kate knows where the condoms used to be. Before it became the thing to use them, she always successfully ignored the little rack next to the till. You have to know where something is before you can pretend it isn't there. It used to be next to the till so people could slide a packet discreetly over the counter while they said in a normal voice that they wanted Elastoplast or Vicks Vaporub, and the assistant could slide the little flat packet discreetly into a discreet little bag. Now they're on a shelf with spermicidal jelly, just below the lubricating jelly and just above the burn creams.

'How much are they?' asks Kate, looking.

The Friendly Local Chemist stands next to her and mumbles. 'Pardon?' asks Kate. 'How many in a packet? Is it always either three or twelve? Are they significant numbers?' There's one brand called Fiesta. '*Coloured* ones?' Kate bends closer. 'Grief, you learn something every day. And ones with ribs on? God.' Vibra-ribbed, whatever that means. There is a packet of four – Perl, with smooth dots. There are Extra-strength, and Prime. Some are electronically tested, which makes her want to ask more questions but she thinks she'll gulp hysterically if she does so she just keeps picking up packets and replacing them, selecting them again. She chooses a packet of three Durex for $3.80 (which makes them $1.26 recurring each), and a packet of twelve Lifestyles for $14.30 ($1.916 recurring each). She takes a strawberry-flavoured packet at $4.95, and a banana-flavoured too. How do they get the flavours in? There are Fetherlite, Extra-safe (so how safe are the others?) and Nu-form (what was wrong with the old form?). There is also one named Gossamer, which even at this moment she has to admit sounds sweet; anyone who chose Gossamer would surely be a gentle, thoughtful lover.

She selects one of every sort Ray Oxford has and builds them into an architectural pile on the counter. The surrounding faces are still trying to be expressionless.

'It's hell being the wife of a health professional,' she says. 'These days. You don't know what they'll bring home. Put them on the account, thank you.'

Ray Oxford stammers. 'You don't – we don't usually – ' He closes his mouth, glances at his assistant, then down at the colourful wall of packets near his folded hands. 'Shall I open an account for you, Mrs Wildburn?'

'Lovely,' says Kate. 'Just use my husband's initial.'

Phew, thinks Kate, as he hands her an indiscreetly large Friendly Local Chemist bag: *Dispatches: first manoeuvre successfully accomplished.*

Back home, Kate leaves Satan to sleep under the oleander, his favourite place. When he's at his most foul-aired, everyone wishes he'd eat the oleander and perish. Kate wonders what the symptoms of oleander poisoning might be. She ought to phone the Department of Health or the Ministry of Ag and Fish sometime, to find out. Amelia might know, though. Barry would. It would be the end of the world if Satan died.

Inside, she hangs the dog lead in the laundry, in its proper place, and sees Jessica's skirt still there. Must be a mufti day at school. Maybe that's why Jessica was taking ages to get ready this morning.

Up in the bedroom, she puts a packet of Gossamer on top of Richard's bedside cabinet near the phone. She opens the packet of Durex and puts one in his blazer breast pocket. A strawberry condom in his light-grey suit jacket, and a Fiesta in his dark-grey suit jacket. A Fetherlite for his green sports coat and an Extra-strength in his leather jacket. And she saves a packet for the coat he's wearing today, and another for his Nike sports bag when he brings it home tonight.

chapter twelve

Kate's playing the piano. Dinner's ready to zap in the microwave when Richard comes in. The young ones are having their dinner now. Oven chips and lemon chicken pieces. With a Waldorf salad in the right-shaped elegant bowl. When the young people leave the table, she thinks, I'll rearrange it to make it elegant again – the perfect wife achieves perfection no matter what, *ha ha*, until she's told out loud she isn't perfect.

She is playing the 'Ride of the Valkyries'. Out loud. Mind you, it isn't easy to achieve total sensurround on a Yamaha upright. You need a full orchestra and several deep-chested women in bronze helmets for the best effect but she can't arrange that, worse luck. In fact, she's never found a piano version of the 'Ride of the Valkyries', though there is one for organ. So she's improvising. *Crash*, *crash*, chord after chord, she imagines it on an organ with all stops out. Actually she's composing. It could be termed minimalist. Whatever. It's magnificent:

Valkyrie: (Scandinavian mythology) a handmaiden to Odin (chief god), on duty in the battlefield and in Valhalla. Valhalla? – the palace of bliss for the souls of heroes slain in battle.

Katarilda calls, deep-chested. Her warhorse strides through the bitter Arctic wind. She swings into the saddle, brandishing her short bronze spear. Her plaits swing too, heavy ropes of flaxen silk wound with threads of gold. Her breast-plate, brass, engraved with runes of victory, makes her invulnerable, inviolate.

Again Queen Katarilda calls. The host of Valkyries, their lovely strong round arms raised high, sing full-throated as the lust of battle surges in their loins, their hearts, their souls.

Out they ride, Katarilda and her Valkyries, while Odin, from his battle tent, prone on his bed of pain (his warhorse nipped his thigh), cries weak thanks that he has Katarilda, his treasure and delight, to carry on the struggle against Evil and Despair. — My glory, my desire, cries Odin, chief god, biting his handkerchief.

Queen Katarilda crushes down a thrill of fear — fear, which but adds spice to the heady mead of battle fever. *(Mead — it's honey and water, fermented — she thinks she'd rather have a cognac.)*

And from the sky, the shredded blues of the aurora, the green of supernatural light, the reds and orange of the passion of the gods, illumine the stern face of Katarilda, the hero *(yes, she means it: hero)* whose fight for truth, justice and the womanly way, will lead unerringly to triumph.

'What the hell is that!' Richard's in the doorway, briefcase in one hand, sports bag in the other. Forehead gleaming. Long game of squash? It's dark outside. A good time for the Valkyries to have a gallop.

Kate has no music in front of her. 'Vaughan Williams,' she says.

'Oh,' says Richard. 'It's very good.' He disappears. Kate

follows. She takes the sports bag and opens it in the laundry. Ripe! Definitely not Opium. It was squash tonight. She fills a bucket with cold water and pushes his gear into it, listening to hear if he's gone to the bedroom, if he's seen the little package by the phone. But he comes downstairs Frowning no more heavily than usual.

In the kitchen, she presses the pads on the microwave and the oven whirrs. 'Lovely day,' she says through the dining room door to the newspaper which Richard, sitting on the window-seat, has open in front of his face. He's probably picking his nose: he thinks she can't tell. She's always glad she reads the *Herald* first.

The newspaper collapses into a noisy crumple. 'Shit of a day. No one knows a bean about my funds. Looks as if bloody Martin will get my share this year as well. I'm due something, everyone else's had more than their whack. But I tell you, it's a mug's game these days. If I did get funds, how am I going to get patients for my trial? You know the patients have to pay to be part of clinical trials in this crazy system? What's the sense of that?'

Kate opens her eyes wide to show sympathy. Not that he's looking. He's never explained clearly what his trial will be, but it seems people will undergo colonic irrigation. It sounds incredibly invasive: Kate can't imagine why anyone would want to suffer it at all, let alone pay for it if they don't need it.

The front page tears under Richard's grip. 'Bloody Martin, I don't know. All laughter, no sense of responsibility. Academics, all the bloody same, think they're better than us, but who does the real work? I know he was back today. But did he show his nose? He did not. Knew I'd scheduled him to give a presentation. Bloody glamour boy.' The newspaper rises noisily again, and the microwave dings.

'Dinner.' Kate talks over her shoulder while she fetches it. 'I said I'd have lunch with Greta. She'll be jet-lagged, poor thing. I should take her a casserole.' She puts the plates on the table and stands in perfect wife position, waiting for Richard. 'I would like to know her better. Shall we have them to dinner, just them on their own? Or have Tom and Viv as well?'

The newspaper crumples again. Richard's face is lined and tired: he heaves to his feet and pulls the whisky from the sideboard, splashes some into a crystal tumbler. Is that wise after squash? Kate wants to say. But she's seen enough of the Frown tonight. And she's sure to get lots of it later. Upstairs.

He talks about bloody Martin and the bloody board all through dinner. Kate's heard it all before. Bloody Martin was granted the money Richard wanted last year, too. Except to-night Richard is particularly down on Martin. Poor Martin, Kate does quite like him. Bloody Martin is apparently still boasting about getting his century.

'I've had two papers of my own.' Richard stabs a chicken thigh as if it might leap up and run away. 'And I was co-author on three others. And no one counts my letters. Five letters in the *NZMJ* in the last two years, not bad.'

'Mmm,' says Kate, which seems to be enough. She wonders how the Rose in Full Bloom enjoyed Madrid; not much, if Greta was right about what Martin's like at conferences. But mostly, Kate's trying not to be annoyed with Owen and Jessica, who have snuck out leaving the kitchen in a mess, largely to avoid their father who's in a mood they've learned is best avoided. They took plenty of time over doing their hair and phoning friends but didn't take two minutes for cleaning up the kitchen. Honestly, she gets fed up, wiping other people's crumbs. She hopes the other woman leaves crumbs on the motel sheets. That might teach Richard about crumbs, anyway.

Kate reaches for the salt and sprinkles it on her oven chips. Oh God, she thinks, the Frown. She doesn't have to look, she can feel it vibrating at her. She knows she's letting her mind wander because she's nervous about what will happen in the bedroom, later.

I'm not much of a Valkyrie, thinks Kate. Cry havoc! and let slip the dogs of war? Hell, all I've got is Satan. So she eats a lovely, salty chip for comfort.

It's 11.30-plus. Kate longs for sleep. But if she drops off before Richard comes up to bed, he'll wake her. She hates it when he wakes her up. And she doesn't want to be unconscious when he finds the Gossamer. Truth be told, she's too scared to go to sleep. So she's reading. *Pioneers*. Science fiction, about a wonderfully strong and clever woman who is partnered by an equally strong and clever man. It's a novel about partnership and love. No wonder it's science fiction, thinks Kate. After all, the strong and clever man and woman have both been genetically engineered. She is managing to enjoy the story anyway.

The house is very quiet, both kids home and probably asleep by now, so she hears the creak from the study as Richard leaves his executive gas-lift chair. The mumble of Sky Sport fades as he switches off. He comes upstairs and through to the ensuite. She turns a page as he comes out with brushed teeth and a clean face and begins to get into his pyjamas. He pulls on the shortie pants — white with little green anchors — and is buttoning the top over his black-hairy chest when he stops. He picks up the packet by the phone. She turns another page. He doesn't say anything. He just stands.

Kate glances up. 'Tired? You must be.'

'What does this mean.'

'We ought to talk about it, yes.' Kate puts a Mickey Mouse bookmark on page 131. Out of the corner of her eye she sees Richard getting his volcanic look.

'It's a question of responsibility, these days,' says Kate. 'I mean. You never know. I warn the children to be careful, when they get into you-know-what. But let's think these things through. If health professionals are at risk, it makes sense, doesn't it?' She nods at the Gossamer held rigidly between his thumb and fingers. 'I don't see why a doctor's spouse should be a casualty to medical misadventure. I doubt that Accident Compensation would cover it, not entirely.'

She's not supposed to be so rational. He never thinks she's capable of logic. Not even though she adds up their bank statements and finds the errors, and argues with the plumber about what percentage he should charge of an hour's travelling time. That's nothing special to Richard, it's only doing what he would if he had the time. He doesn't admit he'd take five times longer than her to do it, then get it wrong. Though he knows it. She knows he knows it. The children know it, too. But to Richard, if you don't admit something then it isn't true — whether it's true or not.

'Katarilda and the Valkyries' plays in Kate's head as she turns off her lamp. Richard climbs into his side of the bed. She senses him looking at the Gossamer then hears him pull open the bedside drawer and drop the packet in. His light switches off. He's lying straight and still.

In Kate's head: *crash*, *crash*, chord after chord. Wonderful. She ought to write it down before she forgets.

chapter thirteen

Next morning, she feels grumpy too. Grumpiness must be contagious: Richard ought to wear a condom on his head. Kate finds it hard work, keeping cool. It hurts, pretending everything's all right when it's as if she's walking barefoot on a high wall covered in broken bottles and jagged rusty metal. One slip, and even if you don't fall off it's a nasty gash at best, and at the worst it's septicaemia. No wonder she feels grumpy.

'I wish you kids'd clean the damn kitchen!' she snaps. Jessica looks hurt and guilty. She's putting tins of baked beans out on the bench, hunting right in the back of the pantry.

'Mother of the Angry Countenance!' says Jess. 'I'll scrub the cupboards out when I get home. Promise!'

Owen, piling six slices of toast for himself one on top of the other, looks guilty too. 'I'll do the fridge,' he offers. 'I could use a morning at home.' His face is yellowish. Kate puts a hand on his forehead.

'You can't tell a temperature that way.' Richard shoulders to the bench and slams bread in the toaster.

'It worked for Mother and it works all right for me,' says Kate.

'Didn't stop her going ga-ga,' mutters Richard. It's a stupid thing to mutter so Kate ignores it. 'How's school, Budge?' Richard nudges Jess as she's pouring milk, and it slops. 'Don't overdo it. One Brain's enough in the family.'

'What was mufti day like?' Kate asks, pouring water into the teapot. No one answers. 'Jessica? What did you wear?'

'What?' Jessica's mouth is full of muesli. She stares at Kate, blinks, shrieks that she'll miss the bus, kisses Kate's cheek and dashes out with a plastic shopping bag of something banging on her legs, saying, 'Right. Mufti days, y'know how those things are.'

She used to tell me how ghastly Janey looked, how loathsome-pig-face 'Rika wore flares, can you believe it? and why can't Jess have a skirt from Monsoon like everyone else? thinks Kate. She's growing up, how sad. Kate shoves the pantry door shut with her foot. The shelves are a mess and she refuses to look.

Richard eats his toast standing up and passes a cup of tea close to his mouth. He's slopped more milk on the table because he's looking worried at the clock.

Owen switches the fridge off and begins to empty it. Kate is interested to see that he finds the chilly bin, puts ice pads in, and carefully puts all the frozen food in there to keep cold before he does anything else. See, she tells herself, they are good kids, I mustn't be a bitch.

Richard's ready to leave. 'Late again.' Not looking at her. 'Meeting.' There isn't the usual perfunctory kiss which doesn't quite reach her, nor the usual perfunctory pat on the bottom, which usually does. His scalp is patchy, red and white.

What will he do when he finds the strawberry-flavoured in his breast pocket? If it's in appropriate circumstances, she certainly hopes he'll use it. She feels as if her heart's been put in a chilly bin too, but she's damned if she'll let on.

Since Owen's occupied, she looks at the job section of the paper which he is usually poring over by this time. Libby said be serious about it. But there's nothing except computer programmers or escorts. For two seconds, she thinks about giving piano lessons. Hell no. Even when she isn't grumpy, children bumbling their grubby fingers all over her Yamaha would probably be so frustrating she'd want to slam the lid down on their little hands. And Jesus, she's always hated 'Für Elise'.

And financially she doesn't need a job. She has plenty of public activity through her voluntary work. This afternoon it's Remedial Reading at the local primary. The kids don't volunteer. Some of them cry, before they learn that Kate is nice. But the only stories they like are Enid Blyton, and the teachers object because the books are infested with middle-class values. Kate thinks kids should be allowed to learn on whatever holds their interest. And there isn't much wrong with the values as far as they go – Little Noddy works for his living after all, and he's always kind to other people. Mind you, she thinks, that's what gets him into trouble: being kind and naive. Perhaps that's what the teachers really object to. But for herself, she's always hated Little Noddy, he is such a wet. Big Ears, and the naughty monkeys, and the Wobbly Man, and she hasn't talked to Amelia for a couple of days. Amelia will need to be reassured that Kate's all right. She'll go round to be kind to her big sister. Herbal tea and sympathy.

Owen's wiping the interior surfaces of the fridge. He is focused, intent. His tower of toast is still untouched and Kate reminds him of it as she rattles the leash in the special way that signals *Satan's walk*. Satan comes pounding and dribbling.

Out on the avenue, he tries to turn towards Melville Park but she hauls him in the opposite direction. After a tussle he perks up his ears then sets off too hard towards Dominion Road. He's realised they could be headed for Amelia's. But she goes the long way round to fill in time. Never arrive at someone's house before nine, they might be in the shower. Satan likes a romp in Potters Park anyway; a lot of richly pungent mongrels leave their smells there. Satan, a richly pungent mongrel himself, adores it after the effetely aromatic pedigree spoor he's used to nearer home.

It isn't certain, of course, that Amelia will be home at all. But the battle of the condoms must be shared with her sister. Amelia will be relieved Kate's doing so well. Truth is, it's hard work being a hero. Libby's a help but also very bossy. Kate wants Amelia to give her a hug and say *there, there*. She longs for an extravagant cry on her sister's shoulder and hopes Amelia will realise it's her turn.

Barry's V8 is in the drive as usual, and there's another car parked half on the road, half on the grass. Damn. Amelia might have a visitor already. Possibly one of her arty friends because it's a tired turquoise Datsun with double H number plates. Satan howls as she ties him to the tree stump just inside the gate. Even if Amelia's not home, he'd love to sniff her front porch.

She's home. She opens the door still in her dressing gown, an ethnic embroidered cotton thing. Satan barks and sits down to worship.

'Caught you,' says Kate. Amelia doesn't look pleased.

'I'm dying for a cup of herbal.' Kate walks past her sister, down the hall and into the kitchen. A young man with marmalade-coloured hair shaved at the sides is at the bench holding the electric jug. 'Oh.' Kate manages a smile. He might be an electrician, though he could still be an arty friend. But he looks athletic rather than arty, despite the hair. 'Hi,' says Kate. 'I hope that kettle's going.' She hopes that he's about to go as well.

He flashes her a grin of Pepsodent whiteness. He is deeply tanned, surprising in a redhead: he must have worked on it. He is very good-looking in a narrow-jawed way. His sleeveless T-shirt shows his biceps bulging like presents in a Christmas stocking. 'Drystan,' he says.

Oh shit, thinks Kate, and hopes she hasn't said it out loud. Her face has probably said it for her. The marmalade hair – my God, thinks Kate, I've interrupted breakfast! God, she tells herself, I mustn't make that kind of crack, Amelia would never forgive me. She turns to Amelia, who's right behind her, and gives a *really Amelia!* glare. Amelia's gone squint-eyed but she isn't wearing her guilty-as-sin look so Kate must have arrived in time, just like the cavalry. Kate turns back to the orange-haired and gorgeous Drystan.

A grin skitters back and forth like a grasshopper over Drystan's face. Damn, thinks Kate, my oh-shit look has told him Ratty doesn't want to be rescued.

They sit and have a herbal and, while the other two talk lightly about aerobics and music and acting, Kate sees their hands wanting to move and touch and fondle. Barry, what shall I do? Kate thinks. I can't get out and leave them to it. I should do my bit to uphold the morals Mother thought she had instilled in us. Where's my responsibility to my niece, Rebecca? Where does responsibility stop and interference begin? Where's Amelia's damn responsibility to me? I thought she'd be more worried for me. Can't she see I want to talk to her alone?

'How's Barry?' she blurts. It falls like a brick on the wooden veneer dining table. Drystan looks interested, amused. Amelia looks as if she's bitten a lemon. 'Do you want to get dressed?' asks Kate. 'I'll keep Drystan busy if you like.' The tone in her voice has said, *Drystan, piss off.*

Drystan raises his muscled body off the bentwood and taps a muscled finger on the table near Amelia's hand. 'I'll call you,' he says. 'Sayonara, cherie.' Satan raises Cain as Drystan steps into the front garden. Through the window, Kate sees him leap into his car, swerve it round just missing the barking dog, leave a skid mark on the grass and drive off.

'*Sayonara, cherie?*' Little explosions of disbelief want to escape. Kate swallows them: she senses how far sisterly love can stretch. Not far, today.

'He'd only been here five minutes.' Amelia stretches luxuriously and drags both hands through her hair until it sticks out like a chrysanthemum. 'Honey, don't look so shocked.

Admit that he's delicious! You must see why I want him, Kate!' She folds her arms over her stomach, chuckles and moans with a frustrated Bad Girl flicker in her eye. And she still hasn't asked Kate how she is. 'Honey, I hadn't planned anything, I didn't expect him this morning. I haven't even had my breakfast yet. Oh, just think what I could have had! But you wouldn't understand, I know, don't worry. Oh, Kate!' Amelia is smiling, writhing on her chair.

Does Richard writhe like that at the thought of Someone Else? Kate wants to throw a tea towel over the sight. 'I do apologise. You could have been involved with marmalade. On firm organic toast.' Oh no, thinks Kate, I sounded like a prissy bitch, oh shit!

'How come you're so strait-laced?' Amelia's still laughing, though Kate can tell the stern big sister look's not too far off. 'I got all the sex genes, you ended up with all the prudish ones. You'd think Mother Nature could have sorted it more fairly.'

'I hardly think it's prudish!' Suddenly Kate's shaking with rage, so much it frightens her but she can't stop. 'You're a selfish rotten wife and a horrible example to your child!'

Amelia's mouth draws into a thin tight line exactly like Mother's. She sits up. 'Kate. Don't interfere with my love life. Nor my home life, thank you very much. Phone next time before you come. All right?' She stands. 'Don't mess up things you're far too lily-white to comprehend.'

Kate's sister is a patronising cow. 'I understand enough to . . .'

'Barry is my business, and Drystan is my business, and the two are totally separate and I don't need your prissy little goody-two-shoes nose interfering in my life! How dare you try to be my moral arbiter!' She's pointing to the door.

'You're living a fantasy if you think it wouldn't hurt Barry!' Kate flings out onto the porch. Satan yelps with desperate adoration. 'So don't come crying to me when it all turns sour!

107

You're making your own adulterous bed, you can damn well lie and steam in it!'

'You and Satan go to hell!' Amelia slams the door. Her voice stabs out from behind it. 'Just go to bloody hell!'

chapter fourteen

Kate storms to Dominion Road and looks in the window of the Women's Bookshop. Satan sighs, and looks too. They look in the windows of the op shops. They're tired so Kate sits down at a bus stop and has an angry cry. Satan puts his head on her knee but it's not as comforting as if it were Kate's head resting on Amelia's knee. Bloody Amelia.

Back home, Satan collapses under the oleander and Kate sees the message light blinking on the answerphone. She fumbles the buttons to see if Amelia has phoned to say, *Sorry I was such a cow.* It's only a reminder about her next date for Books for the Bedridden. She tries to have a nap on the sofa in the sunroom. It isn't as comfortable as it used to be. Nothing is as comfortable as it used to be.

The phone rings. Amelia! But no. It's Libby. 'Well?' asks Libby.

'So far so good,' says Kate.

'Attagirl.' Libby hangs up. She phones again at once. 'Don't forget to check the bank statements.'

Kate tries to have lunch. The fridge is so clean it's frightening. The cottage cheese and sour cream, the olives and pickles and bacon and eggs, the bottles of tonic and orange juice are regimental in their neatness. She goes upstairs to see if Owen's home to have lunch with her but there's no answer when she taps on his door. She checks. His room smells stuffy so she opens the window. Satan's on the lawn, still comatose.

She's not hungry, so she writes to Alice instead. Then she deadheads the roses, sweeps the driveway and sprays the mealy bug before rushing off to the primary school and the reluctant readers. While she points to words and pictures she keeps hoping Amelia will say, *I'm sorry*. She tells herself that she ought to say *I'm sorry* to Amelia. She wonders what the peculiar feeling is, the one like acid in the pit of her stomach; it isn't quite like anger. The only thing that comes to mind is jealousy, and it certainly can't be that. But someone wants Amelia. Even if it is a just-past-callow youth with stupid hair. And Kate's husband doesn't want Kate.

A little girl with braces on her teeth begins to scream. 'Misss SSmith, Mss-ss Wildburn'ss telling me wrong! That word'ss not marmalade!'

The word is 'spanking'. The teacher takes a look at Kate and recommends that she go home.

And the phone doesn't ring all afternoon.

There are phone calls in the evening. For Jessica. Owen. Three times for Richard but he's late, at a meeting – genuine, Kate knows, one he always comes home from with at least a three-F-FFFrown. People leave messages. None of them are women.

No calls for Kate the next day, Thursday, either. Not until evening. Richard's out. He's got his squash bag, so it must be squash again. Maybe. Anyway, the phone rings.

'Kate,' says a male voice. 'Martin.'

'Martin,' says Kate. 'How was Madrid?'

'Spanish,' says Martin in his laughing voice. 'Dinner, Saturday. Short notice – can you come? Eight o'clock.'

'How can Greta do a dinner party with jet lag?' Kate asks.

'There's a new drug,' Martin says.

'There usually is,' says Kate. 'Shall I bring anything?'

'Hell, no Greta's got a schedule, dangerous to interfere.'

'How is she? Can I have a word?'

'Out at her mother's, giving her a castanet lesson,' says Martin. 'Is Richard there? I've pipped him again, I'm afraid. He'll be none too pleased, but what can I do? Survival of the fittest.' His big-lunged laugh.

So Martin has got the funding, thinks Kate, oh dear, the angst, the Frown. 'I'll let him know you called. He's not in yet.'

'No rest for the wicked.' Martin chuckles.

'Not till it's eternal,' Kate replies. 'Oh, that's wrong – no rest then either, if you're wicked.'

A dinner party. Richard's woman might be there. Kate starts to plan her battle dress.

chapter fifteen

Martin and Greta live in Meadowbank. But it's close to the edge of Remuera so everybody can be kind and say: *The Daneys? Lovely home in Remmers.*

Richard guns his Mazda at all the lights on the way. Kate wishes he wouldn't but doesn't say so because she's determined to have a good evening. She hasn't had a good week. Amelia still hasn't phoned. Kate did phone her, yesterday, but only got Rebecca who said Mum was filming and she'd leave a note and could she talk to Jessica please. So Jess and 'Becca held the phone up for an hour, giggling over Owen's ex-girlfriends which made him so mad he took Satan for a run, and Satan came home tuckered out and wanting cuddles which was a nuisance because he wanted them from Kate. Kate's his top dog, damn it.

So Kate feels she deserves a good time tonight, if possible. She's been feeling absolutely miserable and hasn't seen anyone much. Not since Wednesday when she saw Amelia and Drystan.

She hasn't seen Lyllian Spicer again, and doesn't know if she needs to; she might cope on her own. Bugger what Amelia thinks.

She has seen Owen, slipping up and down the stairs like a wraith, holding platefuls of sandwiches.

She's seen Jessica, rushing like a busy little bee but always with a smile and a how are you, Mother of the Well-Stocked Pantry?

She has seen Richard, over the dinner table and first thing in the morning Frowning at the toaster. She sees him now beside her, driving. Pink-scalped. She didn't see him the only time they made love this week – last night – because the light was off. She was nearly asleep when he rolled over and made love that was quite nice even though he didn't take down his shorties. She thinks he might have worn the Gossamer but it was hard to tell and she didn't want to rupture the moment by asking.

Richard is still gunning the Mazda. She closes her eyes and visualises the bank statements over the last couple of months; actually she took her Deputy's advice and got a print-out for the last little while. Richard has always taken out about $100 cash each week. Lately, there've been withdrawals of $300. For a game or two of squash each week? The money's usually taken out on a Thursday. There was a gap of a week where only $100 was taken out, on his used-to-be-usual day of Tuesday, but there was another $300 this Thursday. Thursdays have often been squash nights: she's going to phone him on an urgent family matter next Thursday afternoon, and see what the hospital switchboard says.

They reach outer Remuera at last and pull up behind the Lingates' Merc. Viv has told Kate it's imported, six years old from Singapore, but Richard isn't convinced it's second hand. Kate thinks he might be jealous, the way he drags on the handbrake and throws open the driver's door. His manner seems slightly tremulous though, as well, so she wonders if his partner in adultery is Viv. Her friend? In adultery anything's possible, she supposes. She wonders what Tom does on Thursday afternoons. She might find out, tonight.

I will enjoy tonight, thinks Kate, I will. She hands Richard the bottle of Shiraz Cabernet they've brought, and gets out of the car. She settles her shoulder bag (quiver of arrows), straightens her tunic top and trousers (chainmail), flicks her hair off her neck (plumed helmet) and strides on her Day of the Invoice high heels into the fray.

The fray is highly perfumed. The house is filled with vases of gardenia. The guests are wearing Fidgi, Poison, Norsca for Men. The kitchen brims with dishes of paella and pilaff, bowls of Spanish custard. When they find Martin, on the patio which takes up most of the Daneys' tiny garden, he's wearing a sombrero.

'You didn't say it was fancy dress.' Kate thinks he looks cute, in a ruffled shirt with a red cummerbund over his round mid-forties tummy.

'Wait till you see Greta.' He takes the bottle from Richard and puts it under an iron table. 'Thank you, lovely drop. Richard, how about that round of golf? Did you know I'm a member at Remuera now?' Richard shows an unusual bounce in the way he stands and punches Martin's arm: *my buddy, my mate*, say the bounce and punch. Then Richard's hands drop abruptly into a stiff-by-the-sides position, like Owen when he was small and had been naughty and just given himself away, so Kate looks round to see if the Other Woman is about. Viv's nearby, but so are heaps of other women.

The men exchange a manly grunt or two, which seems to mean they agree on golf soon, and Martin takes them inside and pours Kate a red wine: Sangre de Toro with the miniature plastic bull still swinging from the torn foil wrapper. On the sideboard is a row of still white: Marqués de Cácres, and another of red, Siglo Gran Reserva, very expensive, $34 plus. 'Oops, I've left a price on, that's show and tell,' laughs Martin. Richard can scoff about that all the way home, thinks Kate.

Richard, already talking to people, smooths his rim of hair, turning this way and that to search the room. Aha, thinks Kate. She tries to see where Viv is now, but can't.

Greta pushes through the perfumed guests, smiling.

Envy sharp as a stiletto slides beneath Kate's chainmail. The hellebore has mutated. Into Spanish. There's a black mantilla over Greta's frosted hair. A big red rose on top of the mantilla. She's wearing a flamenco gown – not a fake deliriously expensive version like the one Kate and Libby saw, but a genuine, passionate dream of red satin and ruffles, low cut, tight-fitting, the skirt scooped higher in front to show Greta's ankles and a flash of bony freckled shin. Kate sees Lana Wilton and Brenda Osbene focus on Greta as if she's a little sparrow (nouvelle cuisine) who has just flown into an alley off a back street and they're hungry strays who'll use any vicious ploy in or out of the rule book to strip her into tatters before they're off for a real feed at the pie cart. Kate takes a quick look at the nearby men to gauge their reaction. Franklin who's-it has a perplexed cast to his eye. Richard has his back to her. Tom Lingate's grinning.

'Greta, that's delicious,' says Kate as no-one else is doing much except going oh, and goodness.

Greta blushes. Which makes the dress almost suit her for a moment. Because that's the problem – a hellebore's too pale for such a costume. The gown screams out for wild black Mediterranean curls, not a frosted shingle cut – not with a mantilla. But the dress, the dress! thinks Kate. My God, I would look luscious in that dress! Even Arnold Schwartzenegger would weaken at the knees! She tosses her long brown hair off her neck, feels for a moment the delicate brush of black lace imaginary against her cheekbones. Then she pulls herself together and feels sorry for Greta.

'Can I help in the kitchen? With the boys off at school you'll be having to cope all on your own. I don't believe a pill for jet lag can really make you feel all right so soon.'

'I've organised a couple of med. students,' says Greta. 'Sweet of you, Kate. But under control.'

Martin comes round with more Sangre de Toro, then he opens the expensive wine and it's time to eat. The meal is entirely Spanish. Each dish has a label in Spanish with a translation. People balance plates in one hand and try to find a spare window ledge for their glasses. Kate winces when people put wine goblets on the top of the Daneys' piano. People exclaim at how delicious it all looks, the *Espinacas a la Catalana* (spinach salad with pine nuts & anchovies), the *Chilli con Carne* (chilli, non-vegetarian). People exclaim at how delicious it all tastes, the *Paté de Cabracho* (fish paté), the *Pollo Extremeño* (chicken in red wine). They're ecstatic about the *paella* (paella). Kate's head buzzes. People make jokes to William the renal surgeon about the *riñonada* in pepper sauce. They make jokes to Alison the endocrinologist about the *lechecillas* in prawn sauce. Kate wonders how Richard could possibly have an affair with any of these people. Everyone makes a version of the same joke: Martin and Greta will have to do this each time they come back, can they go to Venice/Paris/Tokyo next? People joke about a floor show: is there a troupe of gypsies waiting out back to give a rousing exhibition of the tarantella, fandango, sarabande?

Martin and Greta exchange glances, with Greta blushing on and off like a security lamp. Kate tries talking to Tom Lingate to judge whether the rumours about him are true, which could be a reason for Viv being interested in Richard, though Kate thinks that to switch from a medical spouse to a medical lover would be swapping a battered frying pan for a worse than fitful fire. But it's hard to pay attention. People sit on the floor, perch on the backs of sofas, lean on the piano. Every time things settle, someone else is off on another expedition for more pilaff. Then there's dessert: *Tarta de Santiaga* (egg & almond tart), *Higos y Arroz* (figs & rice). The *Buñuelos de Plãctano* (banana fritters) are divine. And there are all those bowls of custard. Actually, Kate feels sick. Richard's in the conservatory. She can't see who he's with, without seeming like an anxious wife whose husband might be having an affair. But she did hear that rumour about Viv once, and there she is arguing with Brenda at the conservatory door. Kate tries to keep her head turned that way, to gather clues.

The students begin collecting empty plates. Kate recognises one from some other function. This particular young woman seems nervous, exactly as Kate knows Alice does if she has to circulate among people who make her feel inferior.

No one's saying thank you to the students. Kate makes a little face at the young woman: *Don't take us seriously, for God's sake, I know we're awful.* The student is startled into a giggle. As Kate hands over her plate, she and the student both say thank you at the same time. The girl looks happier, more relaxed. A shock wave flutters in Kate's stomach — a student? thinks Kate, is that why she looked nervous, is Richard having an affair with her?

Tom Lingate's watching Kate. 'That was nice,' he says in a surprisingly non-threatening way for Tom.

She stares at him, tries to calm down. No, Richard couldn't, she thinks. And Tom is so non-threatening that she asks, 'What do you do, Thursday afternoons?'

One of his eyebrows disappears under his fringe like a hairy caterpillar under a cineraria leaf. The Lingate grin comes back. He bends closer. 'Nice earrings, Kate.' It surprises her. Not that he likes the earrings, but the change in his voice. Animal low, with meaning in it.

Grief! she thinks, is it true that the Other Woman's Viv? Does Tom imagine I'm looking for a foursome? What's getting into everyone these days now we're all forty-plus? Kate turns away, saying, 'Yes, they're favourites — thank you', and bumps into Alison the endocrinologist. Before she can work the conversation round to find out from the expert if a surge of sex drive in the early-middle-aged is normal, Martin calls for attention.

'*¡Olé!*' He sticks out a hip and stamps his feet.

'*¡Olé!*' shouts everyone else. Kate wishes she hadn't come after all.

'Clear the floor, *por favor*.' He shoos people until a space is cleared in the middle of the living room. Kate sees Richard now, just behind Viv Lingate. Viv whispers to the woman next to her. They give naughty I've-guessed-what's-next smiles: to Kate, it doesn't seem as if Viv is the least interested in Richard and he's looking the other way, back into the dining room. And that student was sweet but also young and clumsy. Not what Kate would have imagined as Richard's taste at all. Puzzling.

'Now you'll pay for your meal, *hombres*,' says Martin, crossing to the piano. 'You have to put up with my playing – '

Cries of '*¡Maldito!*' '*¡Vomito!*' '*¡Bastar ya!*' and someone who doesn't know any Spanish puts in, '*Zut alors!*'

Martin opens the lid and cries for silence. He seems to have some sheet music. 'I hate doing this to you, *hombres*, but I've been warned – withholding of conjugal rights, if I don't!'

All the men laugh: **Ha ha ha ha**.

The women echo: *Ha ha ha*.

Martin runs his fingers along the keyboard, tries a few flamenco-style chords, off-key, slaps both hands, palms down. The piano shudders. There are groans and whistles. 'Give me a break, I failed Grade Five!' Martin's weak with laughter.

Someone prods a finger in Kate's ribs. She jumps. Tom Lingate. 'Rescue the bastard!' he hisses.

Martin starts again. It's worse this time. Kate can't bear it. She'd do this better if she were wearing the gypsy dress from Sydney, but she pushes to the piano and flicks Martin's shoulder. 'Out!' She jerks her head.

Martin leaps up, settles her on the stool. In front of her is a piece of music she's never seen before. Shit, she thinks, if I screw this up, I won't see Richard's Frown, I'll get his Stony-Concrete-face, and that's worse.

Quickly she checks how many sharps or flats, and sees that

really it's dead simple. If she doesn't rush into it, though, she'll muck it up — she always does best when she full steams into things. Away she goes. The music carries her along; it curls and plunges, swirling, tumbling. The hot Spanish wind breathing over the Ebro, silver moths in the light of the campfire, stars in the sky. The full red Spanish moon takes all her cares away.

The piano is angled so she can see the floor. Standing beside her, Martin stamps his feet as she gets to the end of the first page. *¡Thum-thump!* And Greta, erstwhile hellebore, flounces through the guests.

Good God! There's a rose between her teeth. Kate is amazed that her fingers don't miss a note. They play as if they read the music by themselves: she only has to glance at it now and then. So she can watch one of the most astonishing displays she's ever seen.

Pale Greta lifts an arm. A foot taps the carpet: *¡tip-tip!* Thin hips and torso swivel, the arms move up and down, the fingers *¡click!* and flutter. Greta's head moves back, and to the side, and to the other side. She keeps good time, at least, thinks Kate as her own fingers slide and pound, twisting in the chords to throw them to the guests, offering crescendos and glissandos. One half of her soul is thrust into the music, the other half enjoys a spectacle that, were it meant this way, would be the wittiest parody. All the adjectives that mean Spanish are subverted: red-blooded is watery lymph, deep-breasted is starved A-cup, full-pelvised, timid-thighed. Aggressive female passion, in Greta's reticent motion, is a pallid photocopy of a first-draft sketch.

As Kate reaches the last two pages, Martin begins to clap rhythmically. Others join him. Greta bends her knees a little more, flings her frosted head and arms a little higher, and stamps a little harder too: *¡tap-tap!* to end the show. The rose between her teeth falls *¡plop!* to the floor.

Applause, and cries of admiration. Greta's hidden in the

crowd and there's so much noise that Kate can laugh unheard. Martin's shouting, 'She had lessons, while I was in the meeting. Laid on by the hotel.'

Oh Lord, prays Kate, I hope she didn't try classical guitar as well.

Tom's at her side. 'What a disaster!'

'I need a drink!' says Kate.

'You were magnificent!' Tom has a bottle of the Siglo Gran Reserva. He holds her glass, his fingers over her own hand, while he pours.

Still wanting to whoop with laughter, Kate wipes her forehead and remembers she's not here to find a lover for herself, the only faithful wife in the twentieth century. She's supposed to see if Richard's other woman's here. But she's having a good time at last. It's nice to feel another man's hand deliberately touch hers, even if it is only Tom. She's seen immaculate, discreet, apparently ideal-doctor's-wife Greta do something that isn't perfection. And people come to say how marvellously Kate played. It's embarrassing. 'It's only something I can do,' she says.

A few start to leave. In case they have to watch another show? thinks Kate. She's desperate to discover what Richard thought of the bloodless flamenco. But of course she can't till they're off home as well.

They take the long way round: the harbour lights are rippling silver spears on placid water. She lets herself giggle and waits for Richard to say something, about Greta, about how pretentious bloody Martin is, but he's silent, as if he's sad.

'Wasn't it marvellous?' she asks at last. 'Can you believe she had the nerve? Can you believe she didn't see how – how – ' She giggles again, unable to finish. Instead, she breathes, 'I'd love to see what I could look like, in that dress.'

Richard, in a strained voice, replies, 'She did well. I think red suits her.'

Inside Kate's head, a light goes on. A gigantic searchlight, moving, arcing, it points back to the Daneys' house in outer Remmers. It's Greta! Pale, immaculate, flamenco-dancing Greta Daney. The image of Greta's face alive with urgent passion on some motel sheets? It just won't materialise in Kate's mind at all. But it's her. It's Greta. Hellebore.

God help me, thinks Kate. I'll have to keep my second appointment with the counsellor after all.

chapter sixteen

Kate has never known before how totally awful a person can feel. While Richard's having his morning shower she lets the awful feelings surface for a moment. What a thoroughly pleasant life she's had till now. She's always known that someone loves her, needs her. Richard needed her to cope with the kids and Satan. Amelia loved her before Kate screwed things up last week. Her mother loved her, before she went senile.

But now I might, at last, be forced to discover what it's like to have no one to love me except Alice, Owen, Jessica and you can't count Satan, she thinks. Because if Richard's in love with Greta, he might not love me. It can't be lust, or adventure, or intrigue or a power kick or anything but love – can it? Because Greta immaculate Daney couldn't possibly be lustful, or adventurous, or intriguing; she proved that in her mousy flamenco. So Richard must be in love with her.

Love is completely inexplicable 💣

thinks Kate.

All night long, she has nearly dropped off to sleep on her designer fabric deep-quilted posture-perfect total suspension queensize mattress and base, and her Supersleep Soft pillow which is great for people with long necks and is meant to give her a solid night's rest. But she kept being jerked awake as if a giant hand grabbed her by the ribcage and yanked her back out of a pit. Sleep, instead of soothing and comforting, has battered and mauled, ripped her open and crumpled her up. Last night's Sangre de Toro mixed with the Siglo Gran Reserva isn't helping, either.

She struggles into her dressing gown. Shit, she thinks when she catches sight of herself in the mirror. The Warrior Queen after a hard night. Her forehead is corrugated like a desert of stones. Dark gullies lie under her eyes and down the sides of her nose. Crates of suffering have been smuggled into the set of her mouth; they prop up the column of her throat, the texture of which is arid Cordillera Cantabrica, dried out by the red Spanish sun and all those campfires.

'Thanks a lot,' she mumbles at all the gold-topped bottles and tubes on the dressing table. Skin toner, moisture creme, eye-care concentrate, the light-and-natural foundation, blushers, lipsticks, the eye shadows, mascaras, eyeliners. 'Load of crap,' she mutters at the dish of plastic bubbles that look like embryos and are meant, when you break them open and dab the oil on every day for three months, then twice a week forevermore, to preserve your under-eye skin. There is, at a rough guess, over $500 worth of make-up. She can't even do quick sums in her head, she feels so terrible. So terrible she can't even cry – thank goodness, because then what would she say to Richard? None of it has helped. None of that con-man sweet-smelling crap has helped her to look better on this, the worst morning of her life. Because none of it has helped keep her husband from looking at, from screwing and falling in love with, Greta Daney.

Richard comes out of the ensuite.

'I will never buy another woman's magazine,' says Kate, sounding strangled as she stumbles from the bedroom. There is a glance of puzzlement from Richard, which she ignores. Why tell him the journalists who write *How To Keep Your Man Interested* and *How To Grow Older Beautifully* and *How Not to*

Be Fat at Forty have got it wrong. They're living in the clouds.

She descends the stairs: Mary Queen of Scots on her way to the chopping block. She enters the kitchen and chops dog roll for Satan. He shouldn't have any till evening but Satan, no matter how old and smelly he becomes, will always love her, no matter how old and smelly she becomes. Kate slips bread into the toaster. Drops of water sizzle somewhere. Tears at last, and bread, both toasting.

Kate realises she's back where she started when she first found the invoice. Like that poor frog that's always trying to climb out of the well. She's slipped right back down, past her false strength, below the fake determination, down the slimy wall into the mucky puddle of feeling unloved at the bottom.

She also realises, when she hears the nearby church bell dong and make Satan howl as it always does, that it's Sunday and she didn't have to get up yet at all.

Kate feels sorry for herself all Sunday. On Monday, alone in the kitchen after Richard and Owen and Jessica and Satan have disappeared to work, job-hunting, school and the oleander bush, Kate watches more tears dripping silently onto the bench between the crumbs. Amelia's tears spurt, she thinks, but mine just drip. She moves one step along to make a new puddle of tears. The first was because she is not loved by Richard. This new one's for the mess on the bench and floor and the pantry which seems to empty itself mysteriously no matter how often she goes to Big Fresh.

She realises she's not even excited that a new *Enquirer*'s due this week. She doesn't care that:

**Werewolf Rips Leggings off Mt Albert Woman
Victim escapes by shouting Home, boy!
Retired banker found with lycra shreds in teeth**

Kate gives herself a shake and finds the Yellow Pages.

Trust Teleflora, say the Yellow Pages, *trust the sign of the dove.* She phones Fleurs d'Amour and gives her own address. 'Red roses. A dozen, every day for five days,' says Kate. 'Twelve times five is sixty. And here's the list of messages.'

Day One: *With love.* (That's all. No name.)

Day Two: *My dearest love.* (That's all. No name again.)

Day Three: *Sweet Kate.*

Day Four: *Missing you. Please hurry.*

Day Five: *You were magnificent.* (That's what Tom said, and he was right.)

She charges all five dozen roses to Richard's Gold Card.

She makes an appointment for a facial and another for the hairdresser. She makes an appointment for a massage too. A chiropodist. And a manicure, to help her stop ravaging her nails.

Richard's turn. Poor Richard. She hasn't taken enough care of him so he's gone to Greta bloodless Daney for comfort and consolation. Ha bloody ha, thinks Kate, he'll see how much I care.

She phones the city's largest sports goods store. 'Your most expensive set of golf clubs?' she asks. Just over a thousand dollars. She'd hoped for more, but it's all they have in stock right now. Richard's had an old set handed down from an alcoholic uncle who lived and died in Taihape. High time he had something better. 'With a bag and trundler? Yes? Well, I'll have to make do. Can you deliver? And can you accept a credit card number over the phone?' They can. They're lovely chaps at the largest sports store. She knows the Gold Card number off by heart by now.

What else would Richard like? she thinks. Poor man, always so tired after his Thursday squash game, *ha tinkly ha*. She finds Saturday's *Herald* and phones An Alluring Lady from a Classified which promises a pleasurable experience. The Alluring Lady will come and give Richard a massage at 9 pm Thursday.

She is being an excellent wife. She doesn't feel sorry for herself any more.

She also phones Greta. 'Lovely party! Thank you!' says Kate. 'Now, lunch. We said we'd make a date. This Thursday's quiet for me.'

'Oh. Busy. Busy Thursdays,' announces Greta. What a surprise, thinks Kate. Greta sounds as if she's determined to be busy every day for the rest of forever but Kate persuades her to settle on a Wednesday, some time soon, they'll set the actual date later. She hangs up, thinking, and I was going to take her a jet-lag casserole when they got back from Spain. Oleander soup would have been just grand.

Jessica and Owen think the first bunch of mysterious roses is wonderful. 'It can't be Dad!' Jess shrieks 'But he's so bum-awful these days — is he sorry? It's an attack of remorse and sensitivity?'

'A Notifiable Disease!' Owen grins. 'Quick! Call a conference!'

Richard, looking confused, awkward, says nothing. He might think Greta has sent the flowers for him since there's no name on the card. Wait for Day Three, thinks Kate.

The second bunch of roses causes bigger shrieks and grins. The golf clubs come that day, too.

'Uh?' says Richard.

Kate is feeling marvellous because she's just had her massage and the facial. She pats Richard's arm, there-there like Viv patted him all those weeks ago at the Helco dinner. 'You need a treat,' she says. 'Besides, you have to compete with Martin, don't you. There's no reason you can't have anything Martin has, is there, Richard?'

Richard stands very still, looking at the golf clubs. The top of his head has gone red. Red as a Spanish rose. Kate sits at the piano and plays a medley of Iberian love songs. Far too subtle for Richard to appreciate, but she enjoys herself.

On Day Three, Kate has henna through her brown curls for flamboyance: Richard's mother would give Richard a pitying look – she'd pat his arm, too. Kate also has her session with the chiropodist. 'The *tension* in your *toes!*' exclaims the chiropodist, kneading away. Afterwards she feels as if she's walking on a carpet woven of the fluff from kittens' navels. She has her manicure; already her nails are growing longer, as if anger's a developmental protein of some kind. She gets the bunch of roses that says, *Sweet Kate.* The young people still splutter when they see the card.

'Your father's very sweet too,' says Kate in the sweetest possible voice.

'No, he's not,' says Owen. 'I'd worry about this, Mum.'

'He doesn't give me roses,' says Jess, 'and it's my nose he gets up most. If he calls me Budgie one more time, if he tells me not to overwork my teeny little brain, I'll peck his eyes out. But roses? It's extravagant. When there's some people who have nothing, Mum.' What a thoughtful little thing she is, thinks Kate, watching Jessica bite her lip. She gives Jess a motherly cuddle.

Richard starts to wear a double-F-FFrown. Kate wears a smile like the ones you see on the covers of romantic novels, chin lifted, lips parted as if praying for a luscious, crushing kiss. She's practised in front of her mirror. You need to make your eyes go heavy-lidded, too.

On Day Four, she asks Richard if it's squash today. Just to check. It is. Action stations. Yellow Pages. There's a surprisingly large array of Private Investigators, Licensed. Kate's learning something new all the time these days, it's much more educational than Russian night classes, she thinks. 'Can you follow a car today?' Kate asks the Private Dick who answers her first call.

'Just give us the info,' says Private Dick. He'll take a Gold Card number. 'No worries, love.'

Around 1.30 she phones the hospital, but the switchboard says it can't find Richard. Of course it can't, thinks Kate. The operator asks who's calling. When Kate says, he puts a mellow note into his voice. 'Ooh, hardly ever available Thursday, Mrs Wildburn. We thought it was his afternoon for golf.'

'Squash,' says Kate.

'All afternoon!' says the operator admiringly. 'Well, squash then.'

'Silly me, I thought today was Wednesday,' says Kate. 'Do you have days like that?'

'Oh, all the time,' breathes the mellow-voiced operator. 'Have you tried his cell phone?'

'I couldn't,' says Kate. 'It might put him off his stroke.'

'That's really considerate,' breathes the operator. Kate thinks he's a darling.

Next she calls the hospital where Martin works. It sounds like the same operator. 'Professor Daney? Is he around today? This is Mr Wildburn's wife, I can't get hold of Mrs Daney or my husband and I need to check a time... '

'Oh no! Prof. D. does a clinic in the outskirts, every Thursday pm. One to six or later. It's a biggie.' The operator sounds proud to know the details.

Good, thinks Kate. I'm right. But I did want the hospitals to know that what they probably suspect is going on, is going on, and that I know it too. As well as trusting Teleflora, she trusts the interconnecting hospital grapevines.

❀ *Trust is a beautiful thing* ❀

she thinks.

At two in the afternoon, Private Dick phones back as promised. He gives her an address. She feels something lurch beneath her heart. 'Thank you. I may need the same next week,' says Kate.

She looks in the mirror to see what the news has done to

her. Her eyes are pools of rage and astonishment. 'Those stupid, silly people. That stupid, silly man and that stupid, silly woman. My God. The nerve!'

'I look magnificent when I'm angry,' says Kate and bares her teeth like Satan when he smiles for Amelia.

Private Dick didn't give her the address of a motel. It's the Daneys' place. Meadowbank. The Remmers archipelago. That's where Richard is this afternoon when the switchboard can't find him. Kate feels sick. She phones Libby, who tries to offer more advice but Kate cuts her short. 'Save it till I need it, Lib. This whole thing's bigger than the both of them. They'll see. Just sit back, watch me, Lib.'

Kate makes more phone calls. To radio stations, and TV. The local women's magazines. The *Herald* and the *Auckland Enquirer*. 'I have information about a possible scandal involving professional people,' she says. 'Their private lives. I can't give my name, but I'm at this address and here's the phone number. You'll have to come before five this afternoon because I'm fleeing the country.' And she reads out the address the Private Dick investigated. As expected, none of the journalists are terribly interested. Except the *Enquirer* one. He *glips!* which she takes to be a swallowing noise of excitement and asks for the address again. She feels no pity. It's tough being a Warrior Queen, but there's no room for compassion when you're on Campaign.

Day Four's bunch of roses arrives. *Missing you. Please hurry.*

Yes, thinks Kate, hurry. She curls up in the sunroom, with a pot of tea and Satan, and imagines:

Greta draws her camisole over her frosted hair . . . Richard waits, a little dribble at the corner of his mouth . . . he sleeks his black hair nervously, The Barometer grows speckled in a growing tide of passion as Greta slips off her . . . The door bell goes. Frustration! (Good, thinks Kate.)

Greta puts on her dressing gown and opens the front door . . .

The TV cameras roll. The journalists' pencils race. The microphones and sound booms are thrust, rigid, in the air:

Shock Horror Sin in Outer Remmers.

Great headline for her collection, if it happens. Even if they only phone and leave messages on the Daneys' answerphone, even if the *Enquirer* journalist is the only one who follows up the tip, it will surely disturb the afternoon of ecstasy. A whole afternoon! From about 1.30 to after 6.30. All that passion, thinks Kate, amazed. Help. I didn't know that Richard had it in him. I don't think he knew, either. He hasn't. Surely. They must do something else.

Richard arrives home at his usual time after Thursday squash. Late. He looks emotionally walloped. He FFrowns at the roses.

'We're running out of vases,' murmurs Kate. 'How was your day? Peaceful? Head down in your agenda?'

FFrowning, he eats his dinner – Toad in the Hole – says things about employment that make Owen slink off to his room to play loud music, says things about small birds and homework that make Jess storm off to play competingly loud music, then staggers to his study.

She calls the Daneys. Martin says Greta can't come to the phone. 'She's had a trying afternoon, apparently,' says Martin. 'Unusual, for Gret. I can't get anything out of her but she's got a migraine. Sure, lunch with you – I'll let her know you called – it'd do her good to chew the fat, dig up all the scandal. Ha ha ha!' He's very nice, and very naive. Kate's glad that she's fighting for Martin as well as herself.

She tidies up in the kitchen, singing: ♪ *If you were the only boy in the world, and I was the only girl* . . . until the door bell chimes. She yells for Owen to hang onto Satan, and opens the door to the Alluring Lady who has six-inch heels and an amiable face. She gives the Alluring Lady, who seems surprisingly unsurprised to see a wife around, $50 cash and sends her down the hall past the handsome but useless grandfather clock Richard's mother gave them for a wedding present. The Alluring Lady and Richard come out of his study very soon, and Richard stands at the front door while the tapping of the six-inch heels fades down the driveway. Kate can tell from his shoulders that he's glaring, though he doesn't turn to glare at Kate. Maybe he's annoyed with himself for passing up an opportunity. Or for not having the wherewithal to take the opportunity, after a pm in Outer Remmers.

'You've been so tense lately,' says Kate. 'I thought it was time you had a treat. I had a massage this week and it made me feel superb. You never take time off to do something nice for yourself.' Still not looking at her, Richard turns but she catches his bull-necked jaw-jut at the roses. 'What . . . ' She brings a hand up to her mouth. 'You're sending them. Who else? You don't think I'm having an affair, do you? God! Richard, you know I couldn't be unfaithful. Not unless I had a really good reason. Who's sending them if you aren't? What a lovely mystery.' She wanders to the Yamaha upright, lets her hands drift over the keys to make them laugh, sits down and punches out a bracket of lusty jazz with the sustain pedal down so hard it makes her thigh quiver.

Day Five. *You were magnificent*. Kate takes a pen and blurs the *were* so that it might be *are* – that's more truthful. She is magnificent. And the message will be just that much more infuriating, since it's obvious the word has been changed in her handwriting.

Owen and Jessica have guessed Kate's at the bottom of it all. 'Ze submarine will leaff at dawn,' snarls Owen, 'be on eet, Mata Hari, you muss live to fight anozzer day.'

Jess whoops, 'Mother of the Mysterious Ways which Really Piss Dad Off!' and salaams on the kitchen matting. They all watch Richard arrive home. They hear him snort at the roses. They watch his shoulders go bull-like and his head go mottled red and white. The kids disappear: loud music time.

As well as the roses, last month's bank statement has arrived. Kate ticks off all the cheques that she wrote out and hands the statement to Richard with his after dinner coffee. His mouth opens and shuts like a groper's. Bending over his shoulder, she runs her finger down the column. At the $673, he gives a yelp. Kate didn't know that gropers yelped.

'Silly me.' She nips his earlobe. 'That was the day I took your jacket to the cleaners. That one with the funny invoice in it.' Richard's mouth closes, slowly.

chapter seventeen

So Richard must know by now that she knows. But of course he won't admit it. Another awful weekend. He will not speak. And nor will she. Private Dick's on hold for next Thursday, in case Richard still hasn't realised just what and who he's dealing with. A Warrior Queen does not give up until the Campaign's won.

Monday. Satan is having breakfast again. Two gulps. Doggy bites gone.

She has to confess, she still feels dreadful underneath her battle fever. She'd have thought it would be obvious to everyone. It's amazing to Kate, and infuriating, that Richard hasn't noticed how utterly miserable she really is. He's behaving almost as usual. He frowns at his toast. He passes a cup of tea close to his mouth.

To Owen he says the usual, a touch half-heartedly perhaps, 'Look at you, eating us out of house and home. Pity you weren't the Brain of the family, you'd have a qualification by now. Mind you, don't know what good it'll do Alice. She'll give it up when she finds a solid bloke to settle down with.'

To Jessica he says, with a tinge of absent-mindedness, 'How's the boyfriends these days. Don't forget your dad, though. Budgie's going to look after her dad in his old age.'

He doesn't hear Jess say, 'Like bloody hell. Where's Mum going to be?'

To Kate he gives a little peck goodbye. He's started doing it again after a break of a few days, though it still usually misses.

Yes, he has been slightly sombre since Thursday, she thinks. Perhaps it was a terrible experience, perhaps there were some TV cameras there. Kate hopes so, with every fibre of her soul (she's sure that's what she's developing, a soul with fibre, like All-Bran).

The garage door rumbles open and the Mazda roars away. She is astonished that Richard hasn't noticed how withdrawn Owen has become. Owen, now piling toast and peanut butter onto one of the biggest dinner plates. Kate taps his knobbly wrists and recommends that he eat another loaf of toast and peanut butter to fill out between the bones.

She is also astonished Richard hasn't remarked on how Jessica has changed too, is no longer a lively, skimming child but has whole hours of being earnest. Growing up. There in the hallway now are her large heavy schoolbags, so many bags for a thin-armed girl to carry back and forth. And far too often there's a line of concentration deep between her eyes before her smile lights up again.

'We're out of cheese,' says Jessica, closing the fridge.

'I bought two big blocks last week.' Kate opens the fridge. No cheese. She shrugs, and drops a kiss on Owen's head as she walks behind him. He's still arranging his tower of toast. 'Eat up, my loves, while we all still can.' The sort of thing that Mother used to say.

Jessica frowns. For a moment she looks like Richard's daughter, which she is.

Owen, head lowered over his plate, says, 'Might be an earthquake tomorrow. Might be a volcanic eruption. Solve a few problems, eh.'

'At least you can eat!' Jessica suddenly bounces on the spot, furious. 'Some people don't have your privileges, fat-arse, selfish pig. You've got parents who let you live at home, you've got parents who'll help you out. You've got a room of your own, you don't have to sleep in a shop doorway! You're a selfish, fat-arse pig!'

Even Satan backs away from Jessica's vehemence. Owen is silent for a moment, head down, before he leaves the kitchen, food untouched.

Kate reaches out to Jessica. 'Darling, that wasn't like you. Is something wrong? Is it the teachers? Or your friends? What's . . . '

But Jess's face crumples. 'Oh, you're so wrapped up in your own life, Mum! What would you know!' She rushes out of the kitchen, heaves up her bags and is at the back door. 'You don't have to know, Mum, if you don't want to know!' she shouts. The door slams so hard the frosted panel cracks. A triangle falls out, smashes on the floor. Satan dashes over before Kate can stop him. He yelps, howls, dances, a bloodied paw held high. He bites Kate's hand before she calms him down. She doesn't care. He only bit because he was in pain. She'd like to do some biting too.

Owen comes running. Kate deals with her hand and phones a glass-fixing person who promises to come tomorrow. Owen holds Satan's paw wrapped in a towel while Kate finds a piece of plywood in the garage. She takes the rest of the glass out of the door and bangs the wood over the hole; she imagines she's hammering Richard's and Greta's heads. She bundles Satan into the car, leaves him at the vet and drives across the bridge. The harbour's sparkling postcard blue and the sky matches perfectly, though it has wisps of clouds instead of sparkles. White-sailed yachts. Warm breeze. Seagulls. Kate would prefer a howling gale, a flock of vultures and the Cordillera bloody what's-its.

The concrete-block moving machine on the bridge is stuck halfway down the city side. Kate begins to cry. When she's across she has to pull over before she can stop gasping. 'Damn it, damn!' she sobs through her teeth, 'I'm meant to be angry, not a wimp.' She gets to the counsellor five minutes late.

'What happened?' Lyllian Spicer indicates the bandage on Kate's hand.

She explains. 'It's worse than it looks. I poured heaps of Dettol over it. Poor Satan was horrified when he realised.'

'Still more concerned for others than yourself?'

Kate gets angry again: good. 'Of course I should care about them!' She rages at Lyllian, storms at her about Owen and his problems with finding work, about Jessica and her sudden mood this morning. She speaks quickly, ferociously, about Richard, 'It's probably only reasonable, understandable anyway, that he should be the way he is, because life's so hard for him. No wonder doctors are so thick at home! The pressure on them! All he wants is to do his research for which there's no damned money! All he wants to do is the right things for his patients, but all the paperwork saps his energy, and when he's normal I do love him and . . . ' She's beginning to gasp again. 'And maybe – maybe he does need someone more gentle than I am. Maybe he needs Greta because she's not as scatty as me. Maybe he wants her because she does look more like his damned mother than I do!'

Lyllian passes the box of tissues over. For Kate is sobbing again, great bites of air, ripping the ugly sounds into tatters. 'I can't compete with her. Why should I?' Does she mean his mother, or Greta? It's all the same to Kate. 'All I want to do is the right thing, for all of them, for everyone I love. I'm a good mother. I'm a good wife and a good dog owner too!'

The counsellor waits with her red lacquered talons together in a steeple while Kate stops the worst of the crying and sits shuddering into one tissue after another as she holds them to her eyes, mouth, nose. Then Lyllian speaks softly, asks calm questions, makes suggestions. Kate can't really hear her, though. She's feeling better for having come, but the answer won't come from Lyllian Spicer, Counselling & Stress Management. It will come from Kate, from not giving in to feeling pathetic and weepy like an actress on the afternoon soaps. She does make another appointment, though, once she's handed over her cheque for $80 inc. GST.

Back in the Chariot, she looks in the driving mirror. Smeared eyeliner, no lipstick because it's been sobbed off. Hair over her eyes. Unbecoming in the woman Odin worships.

What do I have to contend with? Kate asks herself. Greta Daney. How much longer can it last? What factors are there to consider?

Factor One. The Daney kids are away at school and Greta's utterly bored? She likes to fuss and organise and be obeyed. Poor Richard, thinks Kate, he could well have had enough by now. That look in his eyes all weekend − rather like the tourniquet-around-the-temples look he gets when we stay with his mother for more than two days.

Factor Two, she thinks. Greta dresses like an air hostess/ Richard's mother? Conservative, quietly proper. Not a bit like Kate. Well, she's not too bothered. Richard's very ambivalent about his mum, see above, she thinks. And he knows Kate makes a wonderful parrot for dinner parties. He doesn't know she's rattled the bars until they've bent and she's trying to get her head out.

Factor Three. Greta has hidden depths of passion which Martin cannot satisfy? But Martin's an O&G man, he should know about female sexuality − joke, thinks Kate, I've got another joke! Mind you, Richard's a gastro man and he can't help his own dog's flatulence. And if Greta does have depths of passion, Kate doesn't think Richard's got matching ones to satisfy anyone with. Not for long. He just likes the way Greta is so systematic. Maybe they do it by numbers.

Factor Four. Richard is jealous of Martin? Martin has a boat and the Wildburns can't afford one. Martin beats Richard at golf. Martin got the combined funds last year and the year before that. This year too. Martin travels to more conferences and he's due for sabbatical because he's an academic. Martin went to Madrid. Martin's got his century (and deserves it). Martin has his picture in magazines when they do articles on medical glamour issues. All O&G issues are glamour issues. Gastro issues aren't.

Kate is sure that this last Factor is reasonably significant, and she's interested to find it annoys her. She could feel sorry for Greta. If you're going to have an affair, the other person ought to be the main reason, oughtn't they?

Suddenly she remembers New Year's Eve. Greta's little tea-rose face upturned, saying men grow more handsome as they get older, and Richard flushing with astonishment and delight. And *boing* on the clock, and everybody kissing.

Flattery. That's how she got him. Christ, thinks Kate.

What the hell, I am magnificent and I can be as systematic as the next woman and I've got staying power, she tells herself, and drives to the library to raid the feminist shelves for books on assertiveness and the health shelves for books on iridology and aromatherapy and all the things that will drive Richard up the wall with their New Age wanky liberal pseudo-medical bullshit if she leaves them lying round, which she will.

She marches down the Big Fresh aisles gathering the essentials – bread, cheese, dog roll, tomatoes, lettuce, orange juice, pork steaks, new potatoes, snow pea sprouts, eggplant, zucchini, sour cream, acidophilus yoghurt, stuffed green olives, herb mustard. Great piles of Easter eggs spill out of bins. Is Easter nearly here, or are the shops just earlier every year with their seasonal bits and pieces? She buys a couple because they're essential too – Owen could do with fattening up, and this morning it seemed Jess could do with sweetening.

She collects Satan from the vet. There's a bandage on his left front paw. She shows him her own bandage and he hangs his head.

'Could take three weeks or more to heal. I should operate on his bowels,' says Jordan Javinski, DVS. 'Give him another five years. Otherwise – ' Jordan Javinski, DVS and Satan, Doberman-cross, both stare at Kate with soulful eyes.

'Not today,' says Kate.

Back home, she unloads the dog and groceries. He is hugely resolute as suits the sidekick of a Warrior Queen. He is clearly not going to whimper more than absolutely necessary. He holds his front paw high so as not to dirty the bandage.

She settles him under the oleander and phones the school in case Jess is having a real problem and protecting Kate by not saying. Mrs Ferlin is away at a course so she leaves a message, and collects the mail.

A letter from Alice. She won't come home for Easter because she's still fighting with her Teeline. Kate refuses to cry when she reads that bit. Maybe she could fly to Christchurch herself at Easter, then visit Mother in Dunedin. And to be honest, it's just as well Alice won't be home as soon as Easter.

Home sweet home. **Aha ha ha**, laugh all the men; *oh tee hee hee*, laugh all the women.

We'll see about that, thinks Kate.

Miss you all SOOO MUCH, writes Alice. I love you all SOOO MUCH. I sit dreaming of how lovely home is when I'm meant to be writing an article on exciting Cathedral Square which is truly exquisitely boring but I can't let the people down here know. The flat is fine, but my flatmates play abominable music! Country and Western! Ohmigod!!! Blech, puke! I'm longing to be home, and feel comfortable and well fed (don't worry, I am eating well, but I miss Mum's cooking. And a well-stocked pantry! Hadn't realised the great things about home till I didn't have them with me).

Masssesss of kissssesss for you all.

With love love love, ALICE.

chapter eighteen

The glass-fixing person has reglazed the hole in the back door and driven off again. Kate is in the sunroom. Her favourite place. Despite her vow never to buy another women's magazine, she is looking at one. She hasn't bought it, though. It's a *Home & Building* Libby lent her weeks ago but she hasn't had time to read until now. It's all about lino and tiles. Libby's into all that stuff these days, making nice amounts of money out of the eccentric whims of eccentric people. Kate tosses the magazine onto the coffee table, and fishes in the cane rack next to the sofa. She pulls out a handful of old magazines. Do any of these writers know what they're talking about?

What men want from women. No one knows that, thinks Kate, especially not men, why bother ask to them?

What men really think of women. Written by a man. What on earth would he know, he's only one man out of billions.

The secrets of great sex. If anyone knew that, thinks Kate, they'd be a millionaire. The secret probably is that there isn't any great sex, ever. It's a conspiracy and no one's admitting it. Amelia must tell lies.

Chicken drumsticks in oat bran. That looks more like it.

Kate's flicked through them all, cover to cover. The articles on endometriosis, prostitution, sexual harassment, travel, women film makers. The book reviews. The fashion pages, beauty pages, the letters. The cooking pages and the tips on stylish things to buy to show you're with it. The articles on *How to Lose Weight* and the ones on *Why a Woman Should be Proud of the Shape She Naturally Is*.

Kate would like to see an article on: *How To Say To Your Husband, 'I Know You're Having It Off With Another Woman, What Are You Going To Do About It?'* She'd like to see: *How To Tell Your Husband He's a Wanker*. On the cover of a very old one is something about *Sisterly Love*. 'For crying out loud,' says Kate, but she goes to the phone and dials Amelia, fumbling with her bandaged hand.

'Hullo?' A male voice. At eleven in the morning? Not Barry. Barry's voice is so carefully modulated you want to poke it with a stick to see if it can make a normal sound. This voice is smooth too but there are lumps in it. A sweet voice, gooey. A marmalade voice.

'Wrong number!' Kate puts the phone down, burning with anger. Anger at herself for putting the phone down. Burning with other things too. Some of them are irritation, the profound kind, and she lists them.

How dare Amelia be tied up with Drystan this morning when Kate has at last decided to be friends again!

How can she get advice about affairs from Amelia if her sister's too busily engaged in one herself to talk to Kate?

How can she share her troubles with Amelia when by now Amelia is doing to Barry exactly what Richard is doing to Kate? Even though Amelia said it's different.

What is the difference? Kate burns with utter rage. Is it because Amelia says she's still in love with Barry, so it isn't really a betrayal? But that implies Richard's not in love with Kate. Amelia's rotten to imply that, even if it's true.

Is the difference that Amelia only wants an exciting few weeks of illicit sex? But Kate isn't sure that Richard has ever seen sex in the way that characters in novels do – something overwhelming, something to murder for, die for, to cheat and

steal and lie for. As far as Richard's concerned, as Kate understands him, anyway, sex is what men do to show they're real
men, especially if they've been players for Varsity A. It's a duty,
or a genetically programmed thing that they simply have to do,
like grow hair on their faces. Good fun, no doubt about that
(unless Kate's conspiracy theory is true after all). But, well, Kate
has always wondered if there was something about it Richard
was uncomfortable with. Like, why all the foreplay, when the
act itself is − the only word she can apply is 'briefish'. Something to get ticked off on the agenda. It's like all that running
he did up and down the rugby field but he only ever got three
tries (though one of them was a good one). So is Richard
different, with Greta? A whole afternoon? Five or more hours?
Of passion? What does Greta have that Kate doesn't? She still
can't imagine Richard and Greta in a passionate embrace. Greta
probably makes him put his feet up, and says poor Richard, you
should take it easy, like his mother does. Richard would
certainly get off on that, for a while. Then Greta probably says,
now it's time for our belly dancing fantasy and Richard replies,
are we up to that already, good, the schedule's very smooth
today.

   And the last reason she's burning is that the tangle of things
she's burning about comes down to one thing. And it's what
she's been trying to say it isn't.

   Jealousy. Of Amelia and Drystan. Of Greta too, of course.
Oh, that was hard to confess, thinks Kate, I didn't like that.

   So the whole thing's inexplicable, thinks Kate. Fine. I can
still fight. I was brave enough to tackle the Friendly Local
Chemist with my unusual request. Brave enough to slip little
packages into Richard's jackets and brave enough to be utterly
matter of fact when he asked me about the Gossamer beside
the bed. Brave enough not to ask since if he's found all the
condoms in all his pockets yet. I've been brave with roses and
golf clubs and an Alluring Lady and all those journalists. Damn

it, Richard's being stubborn now, that's all. I will be stubborn too.

I will therefore be brave and stubborn and phone my own sister and find out why I'm jealous, thinks Kate. She dials again but it rings and rings and rings. Yes, a late organic breakfast at Amelia's house today.

Kate phones Libby instead. 'I am magnificent. Tell me I'm magnificent.'

'I want to have lunch.' Libby's breathless as if she's rushing. 'But God, I don't know when. There's a mad old man who's dead keen for me to do a warehouse for him – the brother of the mad old woman I told you about. Kate, it would be a plum job, but I wanted to do his home, not a warehouse! I can't handle something so big – I'll tell you about it – ' It sounds as if she's going to suggest lunch sometime next week but then she gives a *squeak*! 'No! Today. I have to see this person first. You too.'

'I don't want to meet anyone,' says Kate. 'I look dreadful. There's a bandage on my hand. I'm not magnificent at all.'

'Slap on a bit of make-up, wear something drop-dead-gorgeous. Meet me in half an hour.' Libby tells her where, and hangs up before Kate can say no again.

At least there'll be a chance to talk to Libby, after they've had the appointment with whoever it is. Not the mad old man, she hopes. She puts on a thin white blouse (from Sydney) and some wide pink cotton pants (Italy) and some purple and pink rattly glass earrings and matching necklace (Wellington, isn't that amazing?). It's awkward to do her make-up because of the bandage. Her eyeliner goes on more heavily than usual, and so does the shadow. She has to leave her hair loose though she'd like to tie it up as she didn't wash it this morning. So she backcombs and sprays it to make it puff up like a bottlebrush flower. Total picture, not like Greta D.

Owen doesn't answer when she yells that she's going out,

so she assumes he's out too. She pops her head round his door to check. Stuffy as usual. In fact it stinks. And no Owen. She wants to open a window, but even though it's second storey, a daring burglar might take advantage if the Warrior Queen's not home. She doesn't think the dog of war would be much help against a burglar, though he might guard the fridge. Reminding herself to tell Owen to give his room a clean out, she shuts his door again and leaves to meet Libby.

The address is an old building, very decrepit. The door is open. It looks gloomy inside. Libby's red Jag is parked half on the pavement. There's a low-slung blue Porsche, too. Kate moves out of the glare of midday into the dark of the entrance. One or two shafts of dusty sunlight come from skylights. Libby's voice calls out, and Kate moves further in. As her eyes stop having to be round as saucers and shapes become clearer, she sees Libby's silhouette and the bulk of a man, round-shouldered, huge-bellied – the one who owns the Porsche? Could be my kind of guy, thinks Kate imagining the huge creaky body squeezing into the little car: that's style, doing what you want, not what people think you ought to.

Libby's beckoning.

She gives Kate's bandaged hand a questioning look and Kate makes an it's-fine face. 'Kate, this is Perky. Perky Lorrence.'

In the greyness, a pugnacious, large old hand moves to grip Kate's. Gnarled, knuckled, hairy. She recognises the name from somewhere. He's wearing a peaked cap like a navvy's and holds a thick walking stick as if he's about to lift it up and whack something. Not Kate's kind of guy at all.

'Libby tells me you're a pianist,' he says in a disbelieving tone. A voice like old spotty apples, the ones that fall off trees and hit you.

Kate blinks at Libby, then at the strange old man. 'Of a kind, I suppose.' He's frowning. He wants her to go away. What the hell's Libby up to? He's got a nose like a spotty apple too.

Not wanting to stare, she glances away. Over in a corner is a shape she recognises. A baby grand? It looks like a Bechstein. 'Who left a baby Bechstein in this dirty old place!' She's probably being rude, and doesn't care. The old man's rude too. Perky's peering at her, head looming nearer. There's a word she's always loved but never used, and now's the chance – truculence. He's a truculent old boor. Squinty little eyes, like a truculent old bear.

'I wanted to be a pianist,' he says. Old spotty apples and pips. Codlin moth too, she shouldn't wonder. 'M'parents said I had to have a reliable career instead.' He holds up a huge hand. 'So I made m'self a millionaire.' Yes, she has seen his name. A property millionaire. Libby's eccentric client, the mad old man. But, a pianist?

Kate eyes his meaty hands. Those fingers would hit two keys at once. Richard Clayderman's got nothing to worry about. 'If you're so rich, why don't you get a piano specially made?'

The old man lets out a growl which turns out to be laughter. Even in the gloom, his eyes gleam, the sharpest eyes she's ever seen, hidden in all those wrinkles. That's what it takes to be a millionaire – self-humour and sharp eyes? Kate can believe it.

'Perky wants me to design a store. A music store.' Libby turns slowly on the spot, arms wide, handbag dangling from a shoulder strap. 'The complete music shop.'

Kate hasn't seen Libby in working mode before. She's tense and smiling, cool. There's none of the manic elegance that Kate so loves. She wants to leave. But the other two seem to be waiting for her to say something. So she does. 'A music store. No money in it. Sure to fail.'

'My money,' says Perky. 'At seventy-nine, I c'n do what I damn well like.' He's frowning again. It makes his belly stick out further, makes him look more like a ferocious bear than ever. Kate would love to see him climb into the Porsche, get stuck and bellow with rage.

'And it's going to be here,' says Libby. 'The shop. I wonder – blue, cool blue. I see the instruments, racks of sheet music, the CDs . . . '

'A music shop with no natural light?' Kate can't stop herself. 'Libby! That's fine for record shops – the murkier the better for kids who like The Cure, and My Bloody Valentine. Def Leppard fans wouldn't care if it were pitch black all the time. But if you're serious about selling . . . How'd you get any light in here! Cold blue? You're begging for disaster – ' Yes, she can stop herself. It's none of her business. She wants lunch and a bottle of wine, a Campaign conference with Lib.

But Libby's grinning now. In the gloom her teeth shine white against the vampire black-red of her lipstick. 'Play something.'

Kate thinks that Libby's as peculiar as her peculiar clients but at least the manic elegance is coming back. The contagion of the weird, thinks Kate, starting to feel manic too. And she hasn't played a Bechstein for years. Even with her bandaged hand, it's something she would lie for, cheat and steal for. She walks across. The others stay where they are. She lifts the lid and strokes the ivory keys; they glow, softly aged. She presses middle C, another few notes, plays a trill, a scale. She makes the piano laugh. It's been recently tuned, she can tell. Perfect.

There's a proper stool, a carved-leg adjustable, well-cushioned stool. She sits down, lowers the height. The bandage won't get in the way too much, but she decides not to play anything they might recognise. And she wants to let Libby know how bloody mad she is with Richard, how impossible Richard and bloody Greta are. After a look up into the rafters of this amazing space, she knows exactly what she has to play: 'Katarilda Rides Again'.

As the first notes sound, the battle surge ignites her veins, she feels the warhorse strong between her legs.

The Valkyries soar down from the dusty cobwebs of the roof. Their spears clang on the floorboards, they rattle their shortswords on their shields. They chant for victory and celebrate their Queen's unquestionable ability to outflank and manoeuvre. She glories in the fire of womanhood which rises through her, up the pillars of her thighs, into the bowl of her pelvis, up through her lungs, her breasts and throat, into the crown, the culmination of her power, into her: *Imagination.*

Odin trembles.

Perky applauds by pounding his walking stick on the floor; he stamps his feet like a bear warming up for the hundred-metre dash. Libby squeals with excitement.

Kate is panting. 'The acoustics! What a miracle of design!' She looks up, to the sides, and up again. 'If you leave the ceiling high and put some baffles on that far wall and the one next to it, but leave the others as they are . . . ' She hears herself talking fast over their agreements, their questions. Kate doesn't know how she's learned all she says to Libby and the crazy millionaire, but it's true and valuable, and so is she.

Mind you, the idea's nonsense. He'll lose a fortune and she tells him so again. Perky's cane goes *thump! whack!* on the echoing floor.

'If you honestly want a total music store, you'll even get people who like Mantovani and piano accordions,' warns Kate. 'I've had enough. I'll wait in the car.' She nods at Lib.

Perky takes her unbandaged hand and kisses it. His spotty apple nose presses her wrist. As he straightens up and looms over her, he points to his nose, eyes squinting. 'Got that in the war. I sliced the chap who did it, though. Other bugger got me first, but I sliced him better.' He goes *skkrrrrt* with a finger across his throat. 'Shouldn't tell you that. Not a nice thing to tell a woman. Bugger that. It's not nice, not nice what you have to do when you're pressed.'

My God, thinks Kate with a jolt of shock, a real warrior. She knows exactly what he means.

chapter nineteen

Perky ushers them towards the sunlit entrance. 'You did a good job on m'sister's place,' he says to Libby. 'M'sister was happy, anyway. Cherubs climbing down the walls. Don't give me any of those fat little poofs.' As they reach the door he grabs Kate's face, turns it to peer right at her, his nose looming a handspan from hers: he smells of soap. She's conscious of her eyes as round as bottle tops with the surprise, aware of her too-bright make-up. But he seems pleased. 'Yellow eyes. I always trust a woman with yellow eyes.'

'Perky's going to want you in on it,' says Libby over the feta salad with huge black olives as large as the first joints of Perky's thumbs. 'It would fit in beautifully with your Campaign. What a poke in the nose for Richard, eh?'

Kate shunts onion rings around her plate. It is an exciting thought but she wants to show Richard he'd better finish his affair, not show him she can be independent. He might scarper with his outer Remmers mistress for a life in Half Moon Bay. It depends whether he and Greta are in love or if it's just a temporary lust. A permanent lust? When hellebore is a purgative and violent irritant?

Kate doesn't know. It's getting worse, not better. And she doesn't want Perky Lorrence to trust her.

On her way back to the Chariot she passes a new *Enquirer* billboard. She stops.

Meadowbank Bondage Ring Crushed
Middle-aged dominatrix darling of local jet set
Ms Spurs & Jelly flees to Barcelona disguised
as air hostess

An all-star classic headline. It will take pride of place in the collection. No wonder Greta had a migraine. Kate sends a silent psalm of thanks zipping through the air to the *Enquirer*'s grotty little office in Eden Terrace. Odin yodels with delight and the Valkyries dance their great white stallions, round and round and round.

'Jessica? What colour are my eyes?'

Jessica doesn't even bother to look. 'Brown.' She's rattling things inside the fridge, school bag tossed under the kitchen table.

Kate has cheered up. She sits on the colonial stool, turning pages in Libby's decorating magazine. There must be recipes in it somewhere. 'Jess, we're running short of plates – have some got broken? Any in your room?' There's no reply except a mumble. 'Jessica? What would you think if I got a job?'

'Oh, Mother of the Startling Question.' Jess laughs and arranges nine crackers, dabs margarine and lemon spread as if she's playing noughts and crosses. 'Why? You going to leave Dad?'

Kate shakes her head, keeping a smile on her mouth, hoping that Jessica won't follow up. Jess, still attending to her crackers, mumbles something: blimmin' pain, he needs a shake-up. Is that what she said? Kate doesn't feel like following that up, either, it sounds like a whole can of worms. There's a thought, she'll do pasta for dinner, with that silver beet sauce from the

Moosewood book, and add some thick tomato too: green worms with blood. She runs a finger over her sore hand. She's been able to change the bandage for a plaster now, it's all much better.

Satan limps into the kitchen: he's heard snacks being prepared. Jessica grins, her effervescent and subversive usual self. 'If you went out to work, who'd walk Satan? He'd start farting worse than ever.' They both look at him warily: he hasn't been walked for two days now because of his paw.

'He could play squash with your father,' mutters Kate, then puts on a jolly voice which ought to help change the subject. 'Letter from Alice this morning. She won't be up for Easter. I'd better check her room anyway, I haven't opened the door for weeks.' A flash of alarm on Jess's face. She must have been borrowing Alice's things. Kate used to borrow Amelia's if there were half a chance she wouldn't be found out: big sisters can be terrifying. She certainly won't tell on Jess. Kate remembers that Mrs Ferlin hasn't phoned back. Should she do something about that? No, Jess has always told Kate if there's a problem with school.

Satan grumbles *nearly-dinner?* and Jess drops him a cracker: *crunch*, dribble. Kate slides down from the stool. 'Don't fill up on crackers too much, you two. Dinner in an hour.' There's no silver beet, so she'll do tandoori chicken. A short-cut recipe. Usually she serves in two sittings, and makes sure that Richard's and her own meal, though the much later one, is as perfectly done as possible. But she'll eat with the children tonight; they've been missing out on motherly attention. And she'll leave Richard's plate in the oven, forgetting about the microwave. If Richard's late, his will be shrivelled. How terribly sad, thinks Kate – sympathetic magic?

It's weeks since she sat with the kids at mealtime. She's feeling odd – miserable underneath everything, of course, because after all, when a woman finds her husband prefers frosted perfection on his agenda to red-blooded spontaneity you wouldn't expect anything but misery, even though you can be furious as well – but now, she thinks, there's a layer of something on top. It was a nice kind of battle today, with Perky Lorrence. Scary, but at least I could see him. Not like the ones I've fought lately without seeing the enemy. What I feel is – not quite optimism. It certainly isn't strength. But it's something like both of those, and whatever it is, it's satisfying. And the chicken smells delicious.

The door bell rings. A courier. With roses. An enormous bunch of yellow and white roses for Kate. For a glorious moment she knows they're from Richard and that everything will be all right.

But the card says: *Join the team. P. L. (and what's wrong with Mantovani?)* Kate starts to laugh. Roses – yellow and white to match her eyes. What a wonderful, intuitive old bear of a man. She leaves the bouquet on the hall table, next to a library book on aromatherapy, for Richard to see when he comes in.

'Do you sometimes feel guilty?' asks Jessica when Kate returns to the dining room. She has stuck her fork into a chicken thigh and taken her hand away. The fork stands up by itself.

'You're not turning vegetarian!' says Kate. 'You can decide not to eat red meat if you like, but chicken and fish are so stupid, surely God put them on the earth for someone else to catch.'

'Just because something's simple-minded, does that mean something else's got a right to eat it?' Owen puts rice on his fork. 'Rice hasn't got a brain.' He puts his fork down and slides a chocolate bar from his pocket.

They're being normal, thinks Kate, they're playing with their food. She looks at her watch; surely Richard will be home soon.

'Guilty at having so much,' explains Jessica. 'It's unfair. Heaps of people never see a dinner like this.'

They're not being normal, thinks Kate, neither of them is eating a scrap. Just then Owen unwraps the chocolate and takes a bite. 'Nor would you two see a dinner like this if your father didn't work so hard to pay for it and if I didn't take the trouble to cook it. Come off it, guys. When you've eaten dinner we'll let our social consciences out for a run. But first up, stop being such a pair of wimps.' She glances at her watch again, and is aware of stillness at the table. Oh dear. Has she snapped at them?

They're both looking at her. Two pairs of dark brown eyes. Two solemn mouths and two deliberately badly done heads of hair. She feels stricken. She's overreacted. She hasn't let them explore with her what they really want to say. Her eyes fill with tears. She ought to stick her head in a bucket of valium for her bad temper. She ought to take a Panadol for her hand, it's sore again. Bloody Satan, maybe she's getting rabies; she'll take a snap at Richard when she's foaming at the mouth.

The phone rings and Jessica begins to scramble up.

'Stay there and eat!' God, Kate hears herself doing it again. 'Eat your dinner, and I shall answer the damn phone and take a damn message for whichever damned one of you it is, and stop playing with your food!'

'Hullo!' she snarls into the receiver.

'Mum!' It's Alice. She's crying. 'Oh Mum, I'm so home-sick!'

Kate can't say anything for a moment. She wants to say, for God's sake, Alice, bug off and let me wallow in my own con-fusion! Instead, she says, 'Darling. Oh, darling.' And after the moment of oh-darling-ing, the funny side comes staggering into view.

'Sweetheart, this is no place to be right now. I'm in a rotten mood, and your father's late again, and Jess and Owen are so mournful these days! And Satan's hurt his paw, and . . . ' She and Alice have a satisfying chat about how awful Owen and Jess are, and how awful it is for Alice. They chat about Kate's argument with Amelia. They chat about the weird old millionaire and his yellow roses. They talk for over half an hour and both of them are giggling when Kate finally calls to the others that it's Alice, do they want to talk? Neither of them answers, and Alice says to give Amelia and 'Becca heaps of love and tell Barry the Brave to keep donging those possums on the bonces, and Kate says she'll send money for the toll bill, and they hang up.

Humming to herself, Kate looks for Owen and Jess to tell them all about it. Richard's voice is coming from the living room. She walks in. Jessica and Satan are standing near the sofa, side by side. Richard's briefcase is on the floor by his right side and his sports bag is on the floor by his left side: this is Tuesday. A real squash night. Richard holds Perky's bouquet like a club, flowers down. Kate's library book is on the floor too. Richard and Owen are face to face as if they're going to hit each other. Burly, thick-necked Richard, more torpedo-shaped than ever, facing tall thin Owen.

'I simply asked if you'd had any luck,' says Richard. White knuckles on the roses.

'It's your tone of voice.' The set of Owen's shoulders slackens.

'How hard are you actually looking.' Not a question.

'I biked to Mangere today. I biked to two places in Mount Wellington. I can't afford bus fares, I have to use my bike to save money.'

'As long as you're trying,' says Richard. The tone of his voice: *What earthly use are you, the Great Mistake.*

Kate knows she does the wrong thing. 'Maybe if you came up with some ideas for him,' she says.

'I will do it myself,' says Owen. His tone says, *But I know I can't, because he thinks I'm useless.*

'Ideas for him!' Richard tosses the roses at the sofa and flings up his hands. Everyone jumps. 'I feed and clothe him! I give him a room! Must I have ideas for him as well!'

Satan growls. Richard kicks the library book and it spins across the carpet. 'What's this New Age crap, are you listening to your off-beam sister again? And what's the game with the bloody roses!' Richard takes a step towards Kate, his shoulders wide and thick. Satan growls again and bares his teeth. 'Get that thing out of the house!' Richard sounds exhausted, strung out. Is that a note of despair in his voice? 'I'm in control in my own home if nowhere else, and it's time you all respected that. I will not have my own dog growl at me in my own house. Lock him in the garage for the night.'

'You're blimmin' unfair.' But Jessica begins to obey, taking hold of Satan's collar. Satan limps, still growling, eyes on Richard.

'What's the stupid brute done to himself now!' Richard sounds disgusted now, head brick-red.

Owen's shoulders straighten. So does his mouth. 'He cut himself on some broken glass. It was the back door. It happened yesterday morning.' Now he looks like Richard too. 'Didn't you notice Mum's hand.' Just like Richard, the questions are more like orders.

'When did you say?' The mottling, the mottling has begun. 'Why didn't anyone tell me.'

Some suitcase looks pass between the children. Looks where things are folded away, not to be examined again, not in public anyway. 'It's fine,' Kate says. 'He didn't mean to.'

Richard's lips are a straight line just like Owen's. 'Will someone tell me what has gone on in my own home!'

'I broke the glass. Satan cut his foot. He got ten stitches. He bit Mum.' Jessica can speak up because she's the baby and he never yells at her. 'Mum, I'm really sorry about the door. I really am,' she adds.

'Bring that dog here!' says Richard.

But Jessica and Owen lead Satan, barking now, out of the room. 'Do I have control in my own home or not!' Richard shouts.

Actually – not, thinks Kate.

Richard stares at Kate as if he'd like to see her stretched out like a stormy petrel in a museum, wings up to dry its underarm deodorant. He grabs her hand, rips off the Elastoplast. It doesn't hurt for more than a second, but it still makes her want to boot him. 'Come into the bathroom.'

He finds antibiotic ointment in the medicine cabinet, sits her down on the side of the bath and rubs the cream into the tooth marks. They're not very red.

'I might have rabies.' Her lips curl back over her teeth: she'd like to make her top lip quiver like Satan's when he smells a cat.

He turns her arm this way and that, presses the wrist and elbow, searching for swelling to see if it's poisoned. He cuts a piece of plaster to size and places it over the bite. He continues to hold her hand with one of his, strokes her forearm with the other, one stroke, then a second. It's tingly: Kate doesn't know if she likes it or if she wants to scream. Maybe she will bite him, just to see what happens.

Kate imagines, in one red flash inside her head:

— You have been unfaithful to me, Richard!

Richard sinks to his knees on the bathmat. — But Kate, it's you I love!

His hand stills. He lets go. He reaches into his pocket and takes out some Durex. Packet of three, $3.80. 'This embarrassed me in front of some nurses today.' His shoulders and neck are thick as a bull's and if he ever charges, she's got no chance. 'I'm tired of the roses,' he says. 'I'm tired of your jokes.'

He knows that she knows, and he is not going to say a word. So neither bloody hell will she.

Richard puts the Durex back in his pocket and washes his hands under the hot tap. 'If Satan bit you, he has to be put down.'

Kate is furious. 'If everything that hurt me got put down, this could end up being a very empty household. But I certainly ought to consider getting rid of anything or anyone that hurt me deliberately. Oh Richard, you're right as usual!'

chapter twenty

S atan must be walked. Even if it's more of a hop-and-stumble, the big meat-coloured intestinally complicated animal must be walked. Kate would rather take up karate so she can pitch Richard into the oleander, she'd rather hide in the bottom of her wardrobe to kick her feet and have hysterics, but she must walk the Doberman-plus-God-knows-what. Besides, her brain seems just as constipated as Satan's poor insides.

The Campaign, she thinks, as she and Satan skirt a bus stop where two late commuters are still waiting with their briefcases and their morning papers. The Campaign's well under way. What comes next in the Battle Plan? I've done the enemy, the terrain – Oh. **Three: the alternatives.** This is the hard part. The choices Libby mentioned.

A divorce? For a moment she wonders why she doesn't want one – anyway, she doesn't. She doesn't think Richard does either. He's looking trapped by circumstances rather than by love or lust. Oh! – she stops walking and Satan sits down heavily at once. Years ago, Richard brought a lab rat home. He'd somehow chopped its tail off, felt guilty, couldn't admit it to the animal room attendants, and wanted her to tend it till it was better. 'Its tail won't grow again,' she'd said. Weird. She ran out of ordinary cheese and fed it camembert. It adored the unaccustomed diet so much it couldn't stop eating, even though it began to look incredibly sick. It died with a very shocked expression on its face. Similar expression to one she's seen lately. Choking down a giggle which she could as truthfully call a sob, she strides out again with Satan lagging behind.

Next alternative. **Fight (dirty).** She's done some fighting dirty. It should have worked. If Richard and Greta have even minimal intelligence they'll know that they've been rumbled and that should be that.

And the winner is – Kate Wildburn! Yay! But if they don't have even microscopic intelligence and do try to keep their indulgence going tomorrow, she will do more fighting (dirty).

Satan leans against a lamp-post and she has to stop again. **Be faithful?** Well, why should she be, if Richard isn't?

So **have an affair.** But I couldn't just pick anyone off the street, she thinks, and it can't be another medical person because they work too hard. If I ever had an affair I'd want someone with plenty of energy, otherwise what would be the point?

Kate feels a jump in the pit of her stomach. Heavens, that was a sexual feeling, she thinks. Maybe I do have eroticism that wants to be unleashed. Wouldn't Amelia be surprised!

Satan decides to pee (difficult, with one front leg un-stand-worthy) on another lamp-post next to another bus stop though Kate does her best to drag him off. A man is waiting there. Kate finds herself staring at him. He looks offended. She feels a blush rise up her cheeks. He seems nice and ordinary, wearing a light grey suit and a tie with stripes, carrying a neatly folded *Herald* and a slim black briefcase. Would he look nice and ordinary without any clothes? Kate thinks that actually male bodies are not terrifically attractive if their bits are showing. If she had an affair, she'd have to see some bits. Which she hasn't done since she was nursing over twenty years ago, not grown-up bits, anyway (not counting Richard's). If she and Amelia were talking these days, she could ask. Amelia, how do you cope with the different bits of different adult men?

A city bus is grumbling towards the stop. The man in the grey suit does look nice.

— I sense your leashed eroticism! says the man in the grey suit. — Let me unleash it! He hurls his *Herald* and his briefcase into the nearest hedge. Kate drops Satan's lead. They hop on the bus, saying, — two to the city, please. Satan whines on the curb, holding up his bandaged paw to wave good-bye.

Side by side on the back seat, they hold hands until the bus stops outside a big hotel. — Unleash me on Floor Six, sings Kate. — Behind the Do Not Disturb sign!

They run, hand in soon-to-be-erotic hand, into the foyer and up the stairs, into Room Whatever on Floor Six. Kate hangs the sign on the door knob. The man in the grey suit pulls the curtains across the windows — the room is dim, the bed looks big and soft —

If he draws the curtains I won't have to see the bits clearly, thinks Kate.

She realises her eyes have glazed; she's still staring at the man in the grey suit. He looks nervous and clutches his *Herald* and briefcase very tightly as he climbs onto the city bus.

Definitely stick with fighting dirty. She turns for home. Satan casts his brown eyes up with utter gratefulness. He holds his front paw high, stumble-hops sideways against her. She staggers and tells him to pull himself together.

Instead, he sits and cries. Kate tugs him. No good. She stands with her hands on her hips. She'll let him sit until she's counted ten red cars. A fire engine races past but she doesn't include that, it would be cheating.

Satan decides to stop playing Hollywood at last. When

they reach the avenue she slips his leash so he can take his own time to limp home. As they near the house, Kate sees a young person, grubby, in shapeless clothes. Waiting for Owen? Just then Owen's bike comes swerving out of the driveway. The young person turns aside.

Owen skids to a halt next to Kate. 'Interview in Mount Roskill. Then I'm into town.'

'Something good will happen.' That's what mothers are meant to say.

He gives a fragile grin, jerks his bike helmet in an oh-yeah? way, heaves his lanky body back on the bike and pedals off. The knobs in his spine stick out like cotton reels.

Satan has hopped up to the young person who shrinks against the fence. 'Don't worry,' calls Kate, 'he's only sniffing.'

She realises the young person might have been sniffing too. It's one of those young ones you see around shopping malls, wearing big coats even in midsummer to hide their plastic glue bags. Though she'll give this one the benefit of the doubt. He-or-she has got the large, suspicious eyes that always make Kate's heart want to break, resentful eyes like those of animals in a zoo. This is a child that needs to be loved, and can't understand why it isn't, she thinks.

She gives the young person a reassuring smile, snaps Satan's leash back on and pulls him into the driveway.

'S'Jess roun'?' The young person's voice is a rusty, glued-up growl, as old and spotty as Perky L's. Kate looks at him-or-her in astonishment.

'Jessica? She'll be at school.' How does Jessica know a waif like this? Kate's head feels constipated again. 'Shall I – I'll let her know you asked. What's your name?'

But the young person, shoulders hunched, shoves hands deep inside her-his heavy coat. Kate watches the figure shuffle away. I should have offered it a feed, she thinks. Oh, the poor, poor little one. But on top of that, she's thinking, how? How does my Jessica come to know a forlorn creature like that!

As she unlocks the door a horrible thought comes over her. But Owen has just left home so they can't have been burgled. Even so, she checks downstairs, ashamed of being so mistrustful. She checks upstairs too. Alice's room is last. Her heart twists when she sees the empty shelves, the closet half full, the room too neat and tidy. It smells of Alice still, her hair spray and shampoo, her perfume and her sweat. Delicious. But as she closes the door, she thinks – no, something is wrong.

She looks again. There's one pillow on the bed, where there used to be two. And the ragged child's eiderdown? Kate had sewn two when the twins were born. Owen's had a puppy on; it went into the ragbag years ago because he used to fight the puppy and win. But Alice used hers for donkey's ages then tacked it up on the wall because she loved the patchwork rainbow and the silver stars for all the childhood years they meant. Did she take it to Christchurch? Kate's forgotten. It's strange, Alice's room without that childhood rainbow on the wall.

My kids are growing up, thinks Kate. I just wish I didn't have to grow up too.

The phone rings. Amelia? Friends again at last?

No. Richard. 'There's a Helco dinner tomorrow night.'

'How lovely,' says Kate.

'Huh?' says Richard. 'Be on your best behaviour. There's a chance they've got more funds. This is important, Kate.'

He is speaking as if she's half-witted. Tomorrow night. Thursday. How considerate to let me know in advance, **ha bloody ha ha ha**, thinks Kate. He has let me know because he'll be busy tomorrow. With his hours-long game of squash. He is still going to play squash, Jesus wept. Her heart squeezes up on itself until it feels as if there's nothing left of it.

*

The Campaign?

Fight dirty on all fronts, no holds barred, decides Kate Wild-burn over her empty squeezed-up heart.

Kate tries to remember to be a good mother, and says to Jessica as Jess is buttering her after-school crackers, 'Don't make a mess, love. A friend of yours was here today. Didn't leave its name. It wasn't a friend I'd seen before. Interesting person, Jess?'

Jessica shakes her hair so it falls over her eyes. 'That'd be Honk. I told him not to come round here.'

'Is he a boyfriend or just a friend?' asks Kate.

'Oh, someone I know.' Jess smiles behind her hair, all sweetness and honesty.

'Is Mrs Ferlin back from her course yet?'

'I'll tidy the pantry but I've got to do my homework first!' Jessica explodes on her long legs out of the room. Soon the strains of the on-and-on scrambly guitar music thumpity-thumps down the stairs.

Kate tries to be a mother again and says to Owen, hunched in front of TV playing with a chocolate wrapping and gazing at an ad for McDonald's, 'For God's sake, stop looking like something Satan's passed.' Owen's eyes snap wide. But after his brief astonishment he appreciates the joke by giving his one-side-of-the-mouth-smile.

Kate tries not to beg for help and says instead to Richard, as they're finishing dinner, just the two of them because the kids grabbed theirs earlier, 'Do you know Perky Lorrence? Well, you won't know him, of course, but you've heard of him.' Richard glances briefly at her. A hunted, force-fed glance, like when he's been in Havelock half a day. 'Perky's offered me a job. Those roses that you ruined were from him. I'd be liaising with Libby. Decorating. Organising. I've told him I'd consider.' She gathers the plates and leaves the room. Richard doesn't reply. Probably doesn't believe her. She can't blame him; two days ago she wouldn't have believed it either. But she sticks her head back around the door and says to his trapped-torpedo shoulders, 'Maybe I could wangle some funds from him for your research. He said he liked my eyes.'

Richard looks like Queen Victoria. A stocky concrete statue. Not amused.

'We could have him round for dinner – he's free on Thursdays,' lies Kate. 'Next week?'

There's a grunt and jerk that means no. For a man who's meant to have intelligence, thinks Kate, Richard is incredibly dense. Fight dirty? Fight filthy, foul and putrid! I certainly don't have to be subtle, dealing with a thicko like him.

Thursday. Unsubtle day. The day of fighting dirty.

Kate finds the picture index in the Yellow Pages and checks under horticultural supplies and agricultural supplies. After half an hour, she's found three places that can help. They promise they'll deliver today. All she has to do is get there with payment by noon. The Visa account will take another beating, but:

All's Fair in Love and War

She pulls on some old trackpants of Alice's, a T-shirt she's used for gardening, ties a dull-coloured scarf over the forehead like a fighting ninja, and puts on a pair of Shadze she hasn't worn for three years. This year her sunglasses are very distinctive so wouldn't be right today at all.

She phones Private Dick to ask if he can do his thing again. She'll call his office about two to check.

She shuts Satan in the house – one of the kids can walk him later – and drives to a chicken farm on the city outskirts. She buys a dozen beautiful free range eggs for the fridge which empties itself whenever she isn't looking, and pays for a trailer load of chicken manure. She drives to a place which has some marvellous lumpy horse manure. And at a final agricultural centre she pays for all their blood and bone. Unbagged. She asks them to take one miniature rose bush with their delivery. A pink rose — too pretty really — but its name is Cuddles which is thoroughly apt. Everyone promises faithfully they'll deliver before four o'clock. She's told them no one will be home. Everyone has said, fine, we'll dump it on the front drive, good as gold.

Kate has lunch by herself in Newmarket in a plain old-fashioned coffee bar, and has sausage rolls and hot chips and tea in a stainless steel pot with a matching milk jug. Soothing. Like having a treat with Mother in the years gone by. At two o'clock, she finds a cardphone and dials the Private Dick. Yes. As she thought. But honestly, it makes her feel broken inside to know how witless Richard can be — doesn't he know when he's had enough? The cardphone spits her phone card back into her hand.

She'd wanted to borrow Amelia's car for the next step. In fact, she knows she ought not to risk the next step. But, she thinks:

if you can resist temptation, it isn't really temptation after all.

Besides:

what use is temptation, if you manage to resist?

So she checks her Rambo-style head scarf and drives in her own car to outer Remmers.

The first load's piled high and steaming on the driveway. When she cruises past the second time, another van driver is pulling away while a truck driver is just about to raise his tray. A perplexed neighbour over the road is holding his nose. Kate senses that everyone finds it strange — it's clear the Daneys' house has very little garden. By the time all three trucks have dumped their loads, it will be hard for anyone to get up, or down, the cobbled driveway, even on foot. Especially on foot.

She turns into a side street and nearly loses control of the wheel. For there is the Mazda MX5. Richard's Mazda MX5.

In the parallel avenue she stops the car and puts a hand over her chest. Thumping, thumping. Not squeezed dry at all, still in the torture chamber, thumping and squeezing. Oh God, she thinks, I didn't need to see that. As long as I didn't see, it was all a sort of game. In the Daneys' own home! It's true! In Martin's and Greta's own bed! It's far more awful than a motel in Greenhithe. The nerve of it. The lack of style! Drystan and Amelia probably can't afford a motel, but Greta and Richard should be able to. Honestly, some people! For Christ's sake shut up and sit still, she tells her heart.

She starts the Chariot again and drives back home.

Satan thinks she smells incredibly seductive after being in all those compost-selling places. She has to lock him in the garage where he howls with lonely frustration. She'd like to do some howling too, with a mixture of fury, disbelief and more fury.

The Helco dinner is at seven. Richard's home by six thirty. Earlier than usual for a Thursday. He looks freshly showered, but Satan (now out of the garage) finds him seductively scented too. Especially his shoes.

Richard isn't talking as they drive over the bridge to Birkenhead. His hands are like steel on the Mazda's steering wheel (that's what he thinks, anyway, Kate can tell).

He doesn't like what she's wearing, she can tell that too.

If you feel you're torn in pieces, dress to kill. A short black skirt, sheer black stockings and high black heels. With a black sequinned top, gold and onyx bangles and sparkly black and gold earrings. She doesn't look the least like anyone's mother. What did that John person call her? Unmistakable.

chapter twenty-one

It's a very big dinner. Helco has taken over the whole restaurant so there won't be any of the people there that Kate loves to watch, the young accountants, the advertising executives and their flashing wallets, and the gold-rimmed business cards being tossed across the tables. There won't be loud chat about yachts and microlights and what a prat Heathcliff was at the PR seminar and what a hoot that Morgana actually got to lay the chief accountant. There will only be the posing of all the people Kate sees posing all the time.

So it is a very important dinner. And Richard remembered to tell her yesterday. She should be grateful to Greta – if it hadn't been for being tied up on Thursday pm's, Richard wouldn't have told her till today.

John thingy comes to greet them. As he shakes Kate's hand, she feels how warm his hand is, large and knobbly. Tom Lingate eyes her sequinned top. Maybe it would be easy to have an affair. But not with Tom. Kate simply can't imagine it, even though Imagination is Queen Katarilda's crown.

One of John's reps offers her a g&t and John counts heads. Most people are here now apart from – he works out it's the Daneys and comments on it to Richard, who does a momentary impression of being a trapped torpedo.

The modesty is rampant. The ack-ack guns are out again: *'When I was on the panel of the blah blah blah . . . '*, *'Did I ever tell you of my rhubarb rhubarb . . .* ', '*My seminal research on yak yak yak . . .* ' Kate sips her gin and breathes thank you to the slice of lemon.

The Daneys come at last. Martin looks dishevelled and he's laughing, lovely man. Greta's mouth is pursed like her tiny red clutch handbag. She darts a tight, pursed look at Richard and Kate sees Richard flush like the dark simmer of Rangitoto.

'Greta!' Kate lifts her glass in a toast of welcome. Greta looks sick. She's probably getting another migraine.

A bubble of glee lodges under Kate's ribs. She is appalled at everything she's done, the fighting dirty. She feels brittle but strong at the same time; she's living for the first time in years.

She turns to John thing beside her, knowing a glow is in her eyes and wanting him to share it because he knows about taking risks, about flying too close to pylons and over kangaroos which scatter and leap.

He gives a little grin, rests a hand briefly on her wrist. 'Excuse me, Kate.'

He welcomes Martin and Greta. Greta's saying nothing. Martin, bless him, is delightful, chuckling about the revolting smelly mistake someone made today, laughing at how every Thursday throws Greta lately, how mad Greta is about it. He brays with amusement every time he says 'manure'. 'And a squitty little rose as well! All that manure for one squitty rose bush!'

Kate wishes that she dare look at Richard. She does. She toasts him too. He gives a look which says: *I don't know what you mean.* Although of course he must. Unless he is completely stupid. As Lyllian Spicer said he might be. With another bubble of glee, Kate asks the barman for a second gin.

Bernard Blaylock, up from Dunedin, appears next to her. In a jiffy Tom Lingate's on the other side, his big hand heavy on her back. Imagination, intuition, flash their lights at her. They know, she realises. Men never used to obviously sniff around, but now they know about Richard having an affair. The grapevine and the hospital switchboards have set up the equation:

Richard playing round = Kate becomes fair game.

So that's the way it works, thinks Kate. Inside, the bubble becomes a pang of anguish. Tom says, 'Got a question for you. About music. We should have lunch sometime.' His caterpillar eyebrows express potential excitement.

Most definitely nyet, thinks Kate. She wiggles an eyebrow back to express I-hope-you're-joking and turns to talk to a passing drug rep – a Clarissa or a Bronson. She's learning how things work, learning about secrets, stratagems, the ways of adultery. She sees the other wives are watching her. So they know too? She smiles, and toasts them all.

The dinner looks magnificent. A smorgasbörd in cut-glass dishes on a purple cloth.

'Sit next to John if you can,' Richard orders. 'Do better than last time. Quick.' He grabs the chair and holds it for her.

'Awk,' says Kate. She awks politely all through dinner.

Kate is strong: she doesn't let people try to weasle her away from John so they can put their subtle and unsubtle case for Helco support. John is strong too: he must know Kate's trying not to laugh, or cry, but he doesn't let on. He talks. Art, books, urban development. Wallabies and kookaburras. There's not one mention from him of drugs or money. Not one phrase to do with medical equipment, not a reference to surgery or health. So she mentions it. She gestures at the food and wine, the well-dressed reps and guests. 'How ethical do you think this is?' she asks, straight out.

He stops mid-sip in a sip of burgundy. Just as she starts to think oh-now-I've-blown-it, a smile of delight appears under his moustache, just for a second, like that animal – the gopher? – that pops out to see if it's springtime yet. He pops the smile down off his mouth again but it still peeps from behind his eyes.

'Ambivalent, that's me,' he says. *Ambeevalent.* 'There's a system, there to be used and I know how to do it.' They look at each other. 'Don't tell a soul I said that.' It's a scary moment, being straight.

'And anyone can learn to use the system?' says Kate with a brittle, furious smile.

'Sure. Use it. Just don't let it use you.' Then he grins, sympathetic and relaxed. She smiles too, an easy one this time.

'More idle chat, I think,' says Kate, her breathing feeling jerky, plungy. He mentions his wife, who stayed in Brisbane when John got the job here: she didn't want to adapt to Auckland. Ex-wife. Ex-children too, because they're grown up and working in Toronto and New York. He asks her about Owen.

'Hopeless. He's trying every day,' says Kate. 'But. Oh well. How big are platypuses?'

John taps a knuckly hairy finger on the table. His sandy eyebrows knit together. 'I can't do anything myself, but Laura Hubbard in PR might. Can I phone you – ' He tickles his moustache. 'No. I'll speak to Laura. If anything's likely to come up, she'll get in touch with Owen herself.'

'He'll think his father's done it for him.' She folds her purple dinner napkin into quarters then into eights then sixteenths and it won't go any further.

'Ah,' says John. He glances at her napkin: her knuckes are white as marble and she quickly spreads the napkin flat. 'You tell him, then.' He fishes in the inner pocket of his jacket for a business card. 'Tell him, ask for Laura Hubbard. I'll speak to her tomorrow.' He writes the woman's name on the back of the card, takes out a slim black diary, makes a note in it. 'The platypus?' He holds his hands about two feet apart. 'They have twin eggs.' He's got lovely blue eyes that really look at people.

Everyone else is moving from seat to seat, and she's feeling hot and faint, just sitting. Time to circulate. She notices that

Richard is avoiding being near Greta, who is sitting nowhere near Martin, who is leaning across a gap between tables saying loudly that Richard's promised him that round of golf, how about Easter, it's time he gave Richard another thrashing. She also notices that Bernard Blaylock and Tom Lingate are noticing that she's noticing Richard and Greta and Martin. She sees Viv watching too.

She is glad she's wearing a short, tight skirt: she has good legs. I will not faint, she tells herself, walks up to Richard and bends over his bull-shaped neck and shoulders. She is aware of his Rangitoto smoulder, of Greta's eyes suddenly turning their way. She blows in Richard's ear. He jumps. Everyone laughs: **Ha ha!** *Ha ha ha!*

Now she crosses to talk to Viv, at a table with Beth Blaylock and Greta. She tells Viv that she loves her dress. She asks Beth about Dunedin, and finds something to say about it – Robbie Burns, the Leith and the albatross colony – because it's Kate's home town. They've all said all of this before at all the dinners. Viv's eyes are strained. Beth looks as if she'd rather be back in her hotel with a bottle of brandy and a video. Kate longs to say out loud, God, aren't these dinners painful? Wouldn't it be a relief, thinks Kate if I could say, we're so well off, we have everything we want except a moment of our husbands' time. But she won't say that while Greta's still around.

So she nods at Greta's outfit. 'Richard would like that. His mother wears a lot of turquoise when she's not wearing clothes the colour of mice or parsnips. I'd never think of putting turquoise and red together, how clever.'

Viv Lingate perks up: that wicked look's in her eye. Even Beth brightens.

'We were going to do that lunch,' says Kate to Viv. 'The three of us.'

'We can dish up all the scandal,' says Viv. They grin at each other for a second and Viv flicks an eyebrow, just a fraction. Aha, thinks Kate, so Greta's confessed to Viv, and Viv doesn't think she ought to get away with it. There's also something in Viv's eye that makes Kate feel that Greta doesn't know that Kate knows. So Richard hasn't told her? Or does Greta play I-won't-admit as well?

'Any more journalists phone you?' Viv asks Greta. 'Funny, that.'

Greta tilts her head. 'Some silly mix-up. Best ignored.'

Oh yeah? thinks Kate. 'Greta, Wednesday next week, come on. You've been dodging me for ages. I'll think you have something to hide.'

Beth Blaylock laughs, 'Ha, ha, ha!'

'I'm terribly busy,' says Greta. 'I do work, you know.'

Kate puts a hand on Greta's and one on Viv's as well. 'I just can't cope. I've no idea what's going on.' She gazes at them with a Satan-pathetic droop in her eyes.

Greta stares at Kate without a smile. 'Why not,' she says at last. 'It might be fun.' She nods, and leaves the table.

Viv puffs out her lips. 'What a nerve! Well, do you need me or not?' Kate shakes her head, not trusting herself to speak in case she screams out what she thinks of Greta. 'That's what I thought,' says Viv. 'Shame. I'd love to see the action.'

'Ha ha?' laughs Beth Blaylock.

3

Cognac

[SATISFACTION]

chapter twenty-two

Kate is astonished how happy a person can be when underneath the happiness is misery that surges into rage like strong slow waves on a stony beach. She is happy because John the marketing manager gave her his card. She sits over her first cup of coffee for today, Friday, and looks at it.

John Colin, Helco Int., Manager Marketing, Pharmaceuticals & Surgical Supplies, Helco Tower and so on. There's his phone number: the direct number, the office, his extension and the fax. There's his home number. They add up to 12,755,154. John Colin. What a nice name, two first names and both could be a surname depending on which way you turn it round: Colin John. And his card is giving her a motherly something to do so she needn't feel so guilty about neglecting the kids these days.

'Owen!' she shouts from the kitchen. It's one of his late mornings. He's overdoing all this biking and needs some extra rest, but now it's ten o'clock. She tells the sleep-soaked Owen about Helco and Laura Hubbard. She assures him that if there is a job, he'll get it on his own merits, if he has any merits that suit whatever Helco has to offer which mightn't, in any case, be much.

'It's prob'ly not ethical,' says Owen. 'A specialist's son with a job in a drug company.'

'No one else cares about ethics, darling. Why should you?' asks Kate.

Owen looks hopeful. Kate's heart wrenches – he may be disappointed again, if Laura Hubbard doesn't want him.

'Mrs What's-her-face from school called last night. She sounded rat-shit. Amelia phoned too,' he says as he drops bread into the toaster. Kate scrambles for the phone. Amelia, Amelia! Mrs Thing can wait; she'll be Jess's mum again some other time.

'I've been a rat again, I know.' Amelia, standing at the sink, pours herbal tea for Kate. She's wearing the coins-and-Z-links necklace, so Kate knows she's truly sorry: it makes Kate's chest fluttery. Sunlight falls through the crystal in the window, making a coloured pattern on the lino, all pastel, like Amelia's floaty cotton top and pants.

'Oh, Scatty-Rat. I'm sorry too.'

'I'm glad you didn't bring your awful dog. Dreadful about his paw, though. He didn't really bite you, did he? God.' She puts the teapot down on the bench. But she doesn't suggest putting Satan down. Kate knows that Amelia, though she loathes the dog herself, is aware that Kate both loves and hates him and that love wins out.

They sit and sip, and enjoy just being together.

'It is fun being a rat, though. Sly and scuttly, sneaking in dark corners. It's all so sexy, hon.'

Sexy. Amelia says the word as if it's blue brie, aged until it runs out of its own skin with ripe, soft succulence. Kate rolls the word around her own tongue: she tastes it, lets it slide down her throat.

'Anyway. I'm cured.' Amelia sips her chamomile. 'Till next time.' She shows her rodent teeth.

'It didn't take long.' Kate's always surprised at this. 'What's the point of having a fling that only lasts a couple of weeks?'

Amelia looks surprised too. 'Why do you always ask?

Because it's a fling. I told you I still love my wee Barry. I wouldn't hurt him for the world.'

'But – ' How can it be anything, without love? It *would* be like doing it by numbers, Kate's sure of it. How come Amelia's meant to know best?

'Even you must've had an itch, Kate. Surely. You don't have to love your mosquito bites, but a jolly good scratch is really satisfying.' Amelia shows her teeth again, and the flicker burns behind her eyes. 'Look at it this way – bungy jumping. Terrifying, but people line up in droves for it. Afterwards it gives you such a high.'

Kate thinks for a moment. 'I'd rather enjoy things while they're happening.'

'Good on you. Richard better watch out.' Amelia chuckles, refills the mugs over at the sink.

'But I'm not going to . . . ' Kate stops.

'So. What's the state of play?' Amelia sits down and folds her hands together just like when they were teenagers. Gossip, delicious, as if it's a cake, licking the icing, sniffing the crumbs. They bite Greta, sample Richard and spit him out, and relish Libby and Perky Lorrence.

'You have to do it!' Amelia exclaims. 'Barry can bring you native trees to decorate the place.'

'It does sound interesting. Maybe I could do it. But,' says Kate.

She tells about John Colin too, how he might have found a job for Owen.

'Honey? Want to try a bungy jump?' Amelia mutters, looking sideways at her sister, rubbing her nose to indicate a set of tickly ratty whiskers.

Kate starts to say no, but it comes out, 'I'd be embarrassed by the bits!'

Amelia squeals with laughter. 'No need! Men are embarrassed enough by their own bits. Poor hunks. God, I could tell you some funny moments.'

For a second Kate's afraid Amelia isn't going to tell at all. But she's a good big sister. 'They're so shy it can be charming. Oh Kate, their bits are darling! But you must never, never comment. Even the most admiring comment, made in the most luscious surroundings, often leads to – ' She makes a downward flutter of her hand. The orange light is glowing in her eyes. The pelvic growl is in her voice. 'In my experience, the most delicious ones are small.'

'Like Barry?'

'No, Barry's huge.' Amelia's offhand. Nature's compensation, thinks Kate, that's kind.

'I wonder if there's a measurable ratio.' Amelia has her eyes closed now, head back. 'I wonder if there have been studies done. You could check in the medical library. The bigger to begin with, the less they actually grow. In my experience. As if there's a maximum size, and each man reaches it either – ' Again she flutters up and down and her mouth goes loose and full for a second or two. She grins at Kate. 'I think all men are secretly convinced theirs is the skinniest, the least, the weeniest – they're sure that other men can do it better, longer, all that kind of thing. It's really cute, the way they protect their sexual reputations so . . . I tell you, hon, the boasting! And they're so uncomfortable about it because they know it isn't going to hold up.' She splutters and has to wipe her mouth. 'In my experience.' Amelia wraps her hands around her mug, then brings them back up, still shaped like a round. 'It's this that really interests me. I should say, these. The best ones take both hands to get around – oh, Kate. 'Cause that means hours of fun. In my experience, that is.' It's as if she's clutching something special, precious, gold, a worshipper adoring something. Kate blinks.

'And Drystan?' Kate is daring. 'With the name like an underarm deodorant?'

'Absolutely gorgeous. Very good.' Amelia is business-like.

'But worried about size, like all of them. He grizzled because I have to spend my one day at the clinic.' The speech therapy clinic. 'Wanted me available all the time. Cheeky pup. And when he told me he couldn't help it, he was a red-blooded male, he looked just like a kid from the infant classes. I couldn't stop myself – I laughed.' Amelia's mouth describes a rueful curve. 'He got so upset. I told him to bugger off, I'd had enough. I can't stand a man with no self-knowledge.'

'Do you have any?' asks Kate. 'Does anyone?'

Amelia smiles wickedly. 'I know what I like. I'm prepared to go and get it. I'm not tight-arsed like you.'

'I am not!' Am I? wonders Kate. 'I think I used to be. I might be changing,' she tells Amelia. 'Wait and see.'

A car swerves up the driveway onto the lawn. It's Drystan's turquoise Datsun. His scarlet hair. Turquoise and red again, thinks Kate. The colours of adultery. I could design a flag: a turquoise Datsun rampant, on a field of clutch purse red.

'Bloody hell. How dare he! Pup.' But Amelia's face is taut, her eyes are wary rather than offended. 'I made it clear, it's finished. I'm not home, right?'

They sit in the kitchen at Amelia's formica table while Drystan knocks on the door. Amelia reaches for Kate's hand. Kate squeezes to show she cares. Drystan knocks, calls out, and knocks again. They wait until he goes away.

Kate waits for something else. It doesn't take long. Never does. Amelia starts to cry. Tears spurt between her fingers. 'I won't ever do it again. I can't do it again. It's just not fair to Barry. I can't take the strain.' She clasps her hands over her belly, still weeping. 'Oh, Kate, it's all so gorgeous, but – ' Kate offers a tissue, and Amelia blows her nose.

'I'd just die if Barry found out,' wails Amelia. 'He's busy confronting himself these days, at money market seminars – "The Riches Deep Within" – when he's not up the kauri. Poor Barry. I'd just die if he confronted Drystan!'

chapter twenty-three

The Battleground:
Wednesday, for lunch. The parrot place. It's familiar to Kate. She needs support from familiar things. *Ah-lo!* says the parrot. 'Ah-lo yourself,' says Kate. Libby's coming too. Kate also needs support from her cohort and legion, especially since Amelia wasn't entirely helpful again. Greta might be annoyed when she realises Viv's pulled out, but she could be pleased to see someone else instead. Kate hopes any pleasure won't last long, though.

She's told Libby to come straight here. She's too edgy to play their Rich Bitch games in the boutiques. As the waitress is fetching the menus, Lib arrives.

'I'm nervous,' Libby says. 'Isn't it silly? But I'd crawl over broken glass for this.' Kate gives her a kinked-eyebrow look. 'Well, someone was after Geoff once, remember?' Lib picks up the wine list. 'I told him if he dared, I'd broadcast it over the office intercom. So I don't think he did. You could use the hospital PR system, have you thought of that? Well!' Lib looks around the little courtyard; the white tables, the other customers. 'Where is she? Chickened out?'

I hope so, thinks Kate, I can't do this. I think I'm shell-shocked.

Ah-lo! Ah-lo! shrieks the parrot. And there is Greta coming down the path, the winter rose, dressed in a pink blouse and a black skirt as if she's a liquorice allsort.

The Skirmishing:

Greta seems pleased enough to meet Libby though she makes a tutting sound when she hears that Viv's not coming. 'No, thank you,' she says to the riesling Libby's ordered. She chooses a chicken salad and pecks at it. Otherwise, she's as cool as usual: isn't she waiting to hear what awful secret Kate needs help with? Kate wants to close her eyes and slide away, but follows Libby's lead. They try to torment, just a little, with small talk about their various assorted offspring.

'I could never have sent my kids to boarding school.' The genuine tremble in Kate's voice suits the topic fairly well. 'They grow up and leave home soon enough.'

'It must mean you have so much time on your hands, Greta,' says Libby. 'I can't stand Kennedy's kids, but at least they keep me busy. Can't stand my own sometimes though, either. What do you do with yourself, Greta? If it were me, I'd get into all sorts of mischief.'

Greta talks briefly about curtain fabric. Kate mentions gardening. 'Have you sorted out that wrong delivery? All that compost – has the smell gone yet?' Greta shrugs and describes the tinted glass in her conservatory and the new light fittings in the hall.

Suddenly Lib becomes a musketeer. She points her knife as if it's a rapier wavering between Greta and a heterosexual couple in the corner. 'D'you think they're having an affair?' Libby nods at the couple: their heads are close together. 'I'm pretty sure. You can always tell. Even if people stay right away from each other – at a party, say – I always guess. Vibrations. What do you say, Greta?'

My Deputy! thinks Kate.

As Greta turns to look, Libby winks at Kate. 'I wouldn't know,' says Greta, chill. 'They might be married. She's wearing a ring.'

'But are they married to each other?' Libby. 'Idiots, really.

Someone always finds out. Geoff, my ex, tried to deny it. But I knew. You always know. Don't you, Kate?'

The Charge of the Valkyries (but not full frontal – subtly done, of course):

Kate rescues her glass from tipping over and sips the wine Libby's poured for her. 'Oh, every time.'

She senses the approval like warm air that comes across from Lib. She senses the bump of shock that happens inside Greta. This could be fun after all. 'There's not much you can do, until it burns out,' she continues. 'I keep him stocked with condoms of course. He's too busy to think of it himself. Can't have him bringing home anything suspicious.'

'It's the nurses who are worst, right?' asks Libby.

Kate keeps steady by sticking her fork into a cube of chicken. 'I just hope they wash their hands properly.' She sends up a prayer for forgiveness to any little nursie bimbos in the Greater City area. She sends out a prayer of thanks for mus-keteer Lib. 'I don't worry much on Tuesdays. It's one of the secretaries that day, and she's quite clean. I pretended I was taking magazines in for the ward and checked her out.' Kate isn't sure if she can keep this up.

'A secretary!' says Greta. 'Not Richard.'

'But it never lasts long,' says Libby. 'Right?'

'Three or four months each year before he peters out.'

Libby pats Kate's arm. 'You put up with a lot. But at least he gets it over quickly. Geoff used to hang on so long I think his mistresses must have ended up screaming with boredom, poor cows. This year it's two women, did you say?'

Greta's mouth opens, but all that emerges is another *tut*.

'The Tuesday one seems best,' says Kate. 'He shaves for ages those mornings, especially his upper lip. And he checks his under-wear more carefully on Tuesday than on Thursday mornings. Isn't the salad good? It's full of capers. I love the spicy dressing here.'

Ah-lo! whispers the parrot.

'Do you have problems with your husband?' Libby asks Greta.

'Hardly,' says Greta. 'I keep him organised. He wouldn't dare.'

Greta's winded her! 'Mind you, you can't be sure.' Kate fights back. 'I didn't know till Richard had been doing it for a couple of years. I think he's got a list of women that he's ticking off.'

'Isn't your chicken any good, Greta? Change your mind and have some wine.' Libby pours for her. Greta begins to refuse again, but then her hand darts out. Kate notes the glass tremble as Greta sips.

'I do think people are entitled to pleasure,' says Greta, her nostrils very pinched. 'If they can't find it at home, well, what can you expect?'

Libby lunges to the rescue. 'It always gave me a rest, when Geoff was playing round,' she says. 'A welcome relief, really.'

'Oh no.' Kate leads the charge. She's Sarah Bernhardt playing Boadicea, she's Meryl Streep and Vanessa Redgrave. 'It's the other way with Richard. He's a tiger. Amazing, how he finds the strength.' She finds the strength herself to utter a tigerish black and orange growl deep in her throat: she wins the Oscar.

'What a shame, you've spilled over your lovely skirt,' Libby says to Greta. 'Did you make it yourself?'

All in all, the battle is a draw. Though Greta is the first to leave.

Four stars for wine and food, thinks Kate, but only two for tactics.

Libby has to rush off to see a client. 'Hey, you've really won Perky over, you know.'

'It was an accident,' says Kate.

'A million-dollar budget. Think what that would do to Richard's pride. It'd be fun, you and me and a big fat million.' Libby checks her watch. 'The supermarket, damn, won't have time tomorrow – I'd better buy Easter eggs now.'

'That's early?' says Kate.

Libby stares at her. 'This is Wednesday,' she says. 'Good Friday's the day after tomorrow. Oh, Kate, you are in a bad way.'

Kate was going to visit Mother over Easter. She was going to visit Alice in Christchurch. But the days, weeks, months have ripped themselves off the calendar unnoticed because Kate's been on Campaign and in a bad way, being a bad daughter as well as a bad mother. God, if it's Easter, her next period's due too. That's all she needs.

'Chin up.' Libby jabs the air with her fist, a combination threat and victory sign.

So Kate is alone in Parnell. She looks across the road, to where John Colin works. The big new building, grey and silver. She should thank him for what he's doing for Owen.

She shakes her hair off her shoulders, blots her nose with a tissue in case it's shiny after the riesling, and walks to Helco Tower. She enters the coolness of the air conditioning and looks at the board beside the lifts. Marketing, 7th Floor. She turns and walks out again, feeling stupid, cheated, confused, feeling relieved as if she's just missed a moment that would leave her undefended. She hasn't even got an interesting fact about marsupial moles to tell him. And how silly it would be to thank him yet, because nothing's happened. Owen has talked to Laura Hubbard on the phone, and will see her next week. Next week, because this is a short week, with Easter. So nothing's happened yet. Maybe it never will.

chapter twenty-four

Kate was meant to go and be a Friend of the Schizophrenics by two o'clock, but facing Greta has been quite enough. She finds a cardphone and tells the dear wee schizophrenic who answers that she's very sorry but she feels too peculiar today. 'I understand,' he whispers. 'So does Zorro.'

When she gets home she's still shaky after facing Greta, from wine in the middle of a hot day and from almost falling off the battle charger. Owen calls out over the soaring notes of his Pavarotti. The person from school's been trying to find Kate again and is more rat-shit every time. It upsets her that she hasn't remembered to let Mrs Ferlin know it was all a false alarm but she can't face a rat-shit teacher now.

Owen also says he's been phoning for jobs but Kate wonders if he's now relying on the Helco thing. That upsets her too.

She tries to find something for dinner. There's a carrot and two mouldy zucchini, a packet of bacon and some dog roll, a scraping of cottage cheese. And, as usual, crumbs everywhere, something sticky spilt on the bench, the floor covered in un-identifiable oddments that even Satan won't clean up. Damn, thinks Kate. A surge of anger threatens to suck her down in its undertow. She grabs the mop, sloshes disinfectant into a bucket.

Jessica arrives home, hair over her eyes, and dumps her bags on the kitchen table. Books and papers spill out. She tromps over the wet floor. 'What's to eat?' She pushes between Kate and the fridge. Satan skids on the damp, flops his paws up on the table, yelps because the sore one hurts, and chews Jessica's bag strap. Owen drifts in with a plate of freshly mangled crusts and tosses them across Kate and Satan into the sink. Kate clamps her teeth shut, keeps mopping. Satan gives up on the strap and tries to bite the dishcloth dangling over the edge of the bench. Jess fetches a stool to see what's on the top shelf of the pantry, and bumps into Kate who bumps into Owen who bumps into the dog who *yi-yi-yi-yi-yi*s.

'Damn, damn, damn!' shouts Kate. 'Out of my way! This is not a communal pigsty! Why can you never get rid of your crumbs yourselves! Take that flaming dog out of my sight while I clean this mess and try to get a meal together!'

Jess and Owen raise their hands in a carnival impression of fear and trembling. 'Momma!' they cry. 'Big Momma's on the rampage!'

'Yes, I bloody am!' she yells. They gather Satan protectively between them, creep out in a way that makes her have to laugh: the stealth, the melodrama.   She finishes the floor and runs her fingers through her hair. She could send the kids out to bring back fish and chips, if there really isn't anything to eat in the house. But the young ones ought to be more responsible in the kitchen. And she ought to try to behave as normal. The Pavarotti starts again, and mingles cacaphonically with Jessica's monotonously rhythmic guitar tape.

She finds a piece of paper and a pen, thinks 'normal' for a while, then writes:

A FABLE FOR OUR KITCHEN

Once upon a time, there were three little pigs. And they never cleaned up their crumbs after breakfast. And they never cleaned up their crumbs after lunch. And they certainly never cleaned up their crumbs after having a snack. And if they did wipe up some mess, they never, ever, rinsed the dishcloth, and they did FILTHY things on the floor.

And Mother Wolf told them she would get **mad** if they never wiped up their crumbs from the bench and the table. And she showed them the floor mop. And she reminded them about rinsing the dishcloth.

But the three little pigs kept on with their bad habits. And there were LOTS of crumbs.

And one day Mother Wolf got **so mad** that she bit off the head of the first little pig. So he could never make crumbs again.

And she was still **so mad** that she bit off the head of the second little pig. So she could never make crumbs again.

And last of all she was **so very mad** that she bit off the head of the third little pig and boy! was it tasty.

Then Mother Wolf mopped the filthy floor. She wiped up her crumbs. She rinsed the dishcloth and hung it neatly over the tap.

And Mother Wolf was happy. At last.

the end

She pins the *Fable for Our Kitchen* on the door of the fridge with a fruit-shaped magnet. Now she feels almost mischievous, waiting for their responses, the reaction of Pig One (Owen), Pig Two (Jess) and Pig Three (Richard). It's a pity Satan can't read, she thinks, or I could have had Pig Four.

It's after six: cheap phone call time. Kate dials Christ-church. Alice's flatmate sounds wary, but says hang on. Kate hears Willie Nelson twanging in the background.

'Hullo?' says a wet kind of voice. Alice?

'Darling, it's me. I was going to fly down and see you over Easter, but it's crept up on me and . . . ' The wet voice has become a gale of tears. 'Alice! What's wrong!'

Alice is destroyed by homesickness. It's rending her into tatters, filling her with cyclones of black loneliness.

Kate manages to make Alice stop sobbing at last. 'Come home,' she says. 'For Easter. Bring your assignment, you'll have time to work. But come home if you want.' A moist, broken yes comes down the line. 'Pack your bag,' says Kate. 'Go to the airport. I'll phone and get a ticket on the Visa. There's a flight about nine I think, and there's always a seat if you pay full fare. I'll sort it out, my love.'

Richard is late home. Kate's not surprised. If he's spending Thursday pm's away from the hospital with Madam So-Calm-in-Adultery, of course he'll have more operations and clinics and ward rounds to do on the other days and Wednesdays was always bad anyway.

Owen has laughed at the fable. He's said, 'Great!' to hear his twin is coming home.

Jessica has laughed at the fable: she's kissed Kate and said, 'I know! I know!' And said, 'Cool bananas!' to hear about Alice. Cool bananas is a childhood joke between the girls and they won't tell Kate what it means.

Kate has found a packet of tortilla chips, a can of refried beans, sour cream, and some chicken pieces in the freezer. There was a lettuce in the garden. She's washed the Slug-slam off it. They'll have Mexican something for dinner.

The Mazda MX5 guns up the drive at last. When Richard

comes in Owen, with the morning *Herald* spread over the floor, says, 'Guess what, Dad!' and Jess, rummaging through the book-case for details about Italy for a history project, says, 'Swee-tart, guess what!'

'I need a whisky first.' The Barometer shows he needs at least two whiskies but Kate lets him fetch for himself – no offers from her, these days. Every little pig for itself.

The Richard pig goes to the kitchen to get some water in its glass. Satan pads through too in case some dog roll might be passed around. Kate sits in the living room and listens. Will Richard chuckle? His chuckle can burst out unexpectedly like a cuckoo from a clock, like it did when he saw what happened to that rat. And because she still likes to hear it, it's a sign they could be all right once he's got over his itch for Greta. No one could itch for long over a winter rose, she thinks. Such a small, pale, organising, unexciting how-dare-she-be-such-a-bitch thing. Kate certainly doesn't like it, but she might allow one aberration in his life. Perhaps. Maybe. Though maybe not.

She hears the cold tap being run. The freezer compartment is opened, ice cracked, the freezer closed. Silence, except for the click of Satan's claws on the vinyl.

Richard appears, whisky in one hand, fable in the other. The Frown. The shoulders. Both as wide and dark as the entire spread of Rangitoto on the sea. 'I suppose this is meant to be funny.' The Concrete voice. My God, thinks Kate, the Frown, the shoulders, and the Concrete voice, he has had one hell of a day. Richard crumples the fable and holds it high. 'I've had enough of your jokes, Kate.' There's a terrible quiet vibrating moment. Then the Concrete explodes. 'E-bloody-nough!'

Owen scrambles up from the floor. Jess backs against the bookcase. Kate feels fear, real fear run through her. Richard's scalp is white, she's never seen it go stark white before.

'I get pressure at work, Kate! Phone calls, demands, all the bloody time! I get nurses and bloody women at me all the time!

I'm up to here with it! I don't need to be a laughing stock in my own home!'

Satan gives a rumble in his throat. Richard kicks Satan and comes across the room, the screwed-up fable in his fist, shaking it at Kate, shouting right into her face. Kate can't hear what he says, she's too damned angry herself.

Satan lunges at the threatening fist and sinks his teeth into Richard's sleeve. He holds Richard's arm down, not wrenching, not biting and tearing. Just holding the fabric, growling.

'Good on you, Satan!' Owen's trembling, fists balled up by his sides.

Jessica is white-faced, indignant. 'It was a joke, Dad. A joke!'

'Satan.' Kate flicks her fingers. After a sideways look at her, he lets go and stands beside her, facing Richard. Jess comes up and holds her hand. Richard steps backwards first.

'I'm getting him put down.' His forehead is covered in sweat.

'You're not!' A chorus of three.

'He was protecting Mum.' Owen steps in front of Kate. 'Hey, Dad, sit down – ' He tries to take his father's arm but Richard shrugs him off, a violent movement.

Jess pushes in, chin stuck out firmly. After a moment Richard lets her unwrap his fist from the fable. She leads him to a chair and sits him down. 'It was only a bit of fun. The rest of us laughed. Have your whisky,' orders Jess.

How strange, thinks Kate, he didn't spill a drop through all of that. How strange, the children seem to be in charge.

'Alice is coming home tonight,' says Jessica.

'Oh God, not the Brain,' says Richard. A weak smile: joke. And a look of shock deep under his eyebrows, that he nearly lost his cool.

'Good, isn't it, Dad?' says Jess with her jaw as firm as a little concrete step. 'We can play Happy Families all Happy Easter long.'

At the airport Alice is still damp with tears, and blotchy. But at eleven at night everyone looks blotchy under the airport lights. Owen and Jess have come out with Kate. She told Richard that he was looking like he did when he'd stayed too long with his mother, and he agreed. He muttered something that might have been sorry. He's deflated and exhausted now, shoulders slumped. So they've left him with the bottle of whisky, in his study with the Sky Sport channel on. They've brought Satan with them, left him in the car.

'I feel ridiculous,' wails Alice as she hugs them all. 'I should be able to cope on my own.'

Kate has a second hug. Her heart tips with joy: the round sweetness of the adult-child's frame against her own, the fluff of Alice's brown hair, the sweat-sweet mingled perfume.

'We're not coping very well here,' says Jessica. 'You won't have a good weekend, I promise.'

'I brought you Easter eggs,' says Alice. She hugs her twin again, and pulls away from him, looks confused for a moment. She wipes her eyes on a shred of white which used to be a tissue and starts to wail afresh, so they collect her case and take her to the Chariot where Satan whimpers with ecstasy at the familiar lick-taste of her face and neck and hands. 'It's so good to be home,' weeps Alice.

Easter. All together for the first time in weeks. At least, they're all at home. They're not in the same room for long. The Warrior Queen's unsettled. She delights in battle – but in chemist shops. By way of agricultural centres. Over restaurant tables – sort of. Not at home. And a Cold War is not exactly battle, either. And she doesn't like uneasy truce.

Thursday is frantic, with the shopping, Alice phoning her old friends and rushing off with Owen to meet people, everyone grabbing their own dinner from the microwave when they find a moment. Richard doesn't play squash. Yes, thinks Kate, Greta said something about her boys coming home for Easter. Good sign, if she puts having her kids home before having a screw. So Greta won't have had a chance yet to bail Richard up about his rumoured other affair with the secretary: that's probably at least one of the badgering phone calls from women which made the Concrete erupt on Wednesday. He seems relieved to be home early and put his feet up in front of TV.

Good Friday Richard spends in his study and the young ones visit friends again. Saturday the same for Richard, with Alice and Jessica working together on homework and assignments, Owen oiling his bike, the house filled with jostly guitars and Pavarotti and now Alice's intellectual local groups on not-very-well-recorded tapes as well. Some Jehovah's Witnesses and later on a pair of Mormons turn up. Kate is tempted to send them through to Richard's study to talk about sin. She calls Satan instead.

Sunday they have lunch together; eye of the storm time again. Very quiet. She doesn't like it. Though Richard is behaving exactly as normal. Lavishing every possible moment on Sky Sport. Spending very little time with the kids and Kate. Making jokes about Mistakes, Brains and Budgies. He's found a new set of blood and gore jokes too, and no one wants to hear them over lunch or any time.

Richard imagines life is normal? After his outburst on Wednesday? Well, yes, because no one's tackled him about it. Eye of the storm, all right.

Satan howls on and off all weekend. Hates Easter. Too many church bells.

Easter Monday, Kate's in the sunroom with an early-morning pot of tea on the table and Satan at her feet. He's sticking closely, these days. Now and then he holds his paw up for her to pat the bandage and say, 'There there, my hero.' She can hear where everyone is: Richard's finished in the ensuite and now he's in the kitchen, Jessica in the main bathroom. Alice is still in bed: there's the faint *knock-knock . . . knock* on the wall which the twins used as code when they were small. This *knock-knock* means that Alice wants a piece of toast. There's a sharp *knock* back, which means Owen is telling her to get it your rotten selfish self. And there's the *rat-tat-tat* which is Alice saying, it's your turn, I got you some yesterday. And there's the full-lunged wordless yell from Owen which says, I'm down the stairs, and it's my turn tomorrow or you're history!

Owen's footsteps pound into the kitchen. Kate finds that she has tensed because Satan's suddenly in his I'll-defend-you posture. She makes herself relax: it's just deep male voices, father and son. The soft *plock* of the fridge door, the rattle of cutlery, the metallic swish of the toaster knob going down. It's good to hear the ordinary mumble of ordinary family life. But Satan's ears prick up, and Kate's ears follow.

She half gets to her feet then pretends it's a cramp in her knee. She shouldn't interfere. But it's her fault, what Richard's saying.

'Wipe it up. Go on. Mother will be *mad*. And rinse the cloth. Go on. Or else she'll be *so mad*.'

Kate's on her feet and down the corridor and in the kitchen, Dobie-cross behind her.

Richard picks the dishcloth out of the sink. His shoulders are wide with I'm-in-command-again, and his rim of hair is glistening with authority. He spreads the cloth between his fingertips and waves it in the air. He turns on the hot tap with a sharp wrench, rinses the dishcloth, squeezes it, elbows out in the flourish of a rugby player screwing off an opponent's ear. 'There!' he says. 'Are we *mad*, or what? Are we *happy*? At *last?*' He throws the cloth at Owen. 'Wipe up your mess,' he orders.

'The fable was my fault,' says Kate. 'It's not to do with Owen on his own, or Jessica, or even just with you, Richard.

It's all of you who make the mess. It was my mistake, to think you'd see it as a joke.'

'There's only one Mistake round here,' says Richard. He laughs: **Ha!**

He pours a cup of coffee and walks outside. Homeowner time, doing-the-rounds-of-the-estate time. The grass is meant to tremble, the paving stones to shrink and whimper, the oleander bush to cower and tug its forelock. Satan nearly follows, turns around in a circle, and sits against Kate's feet.

Expressionless, Owen butters two slices of toast, puts a plate on a tray, pours two coffees. Kate can't think of anything to do that will be the right thing. There's a choice of wrong things, though.

'Well, bugger him,' she says. The reward is a thin flick of a smile at one side of Owen's mouth.

Upstairs, a shriek rings out. Alice's door bangs open. 'What's happened to my quilt!' she yells. 'Mum! Did you give my quilt to the Salvation Army?' She's running down the stairs. 'I thought something was weird! All weekend. I couldn't figure it out. Mum, the Sallies don't need my quilt!'

'I thought you took it with you,' says Kate.

'I wouldn't take a baby thing to Christchurch.' Twenty-year-old scorn. But she wants her baby thing at home, thinks Kate.

'Ask Jess.' Owen thrusts a piece of toast at Alice.

Alice grabs it, begins to chew. 'Jessica!' she yells. Crumbs of toast fall and Satan licks them up.

But when Jessica arrives, hair wrapped in a bath towel, she claims innocence. Claims it rather well, thinks Kate – probably is to do with her after all, so what happened to the missing pillow?

'Jess,' says Owen, warning, with a note of Richard in his voice.

Jessica's mouth goes straight and so do her shoulders. 'Ask

Owen. He's such a kid these days.' She and Owen exchange glances. Kate can't understand why he doesn't protest. He wouldn't have the quilt, but why does he look at Jess that way? Has some kind of deal been made between those two? Unspoken, hidden-in-a-suitcase deal?

Alice gives a nonchalant shrug but Kate can tell she's hurt, not just at the disappearance of the quilt but at the no-speak front of Jess and Owen. 'Where's your own toast, O? That's not enough for all of us. Come on,' Alice says. 'Brekkie in your room, O.'

'No, yours.' Owen's flushing.

'You! Have so got my bloody quilt!' Alice dashes out and slams the door. Owen shouts, trips over Satan, drops the tray and leaves it as he crashes after Alice.

'Shit!' says Jessica. Kate agrees. They follow, leaving Satan to revel in the dropped breakfast.

The twins are wrestling at the top of the stairs. Alice breaks free and flings Owen's door wide. 'What a stink!' she cries. She throws herself at the wardrobe, hurls clothes out.

Owen tries to stop her, but Kate has his arm now. 'Calm down, calm down.'

Jess is the undersong: 'Shit. Oh shit. Oh shit.'

Alice pulls the duvet off the bed: no quilt. She collapses onto her knees to peer beneath the base. 'What the hell have you – ' There's a quiet gasp, then slowly she turns and stares at Owen.

The fight goes out of him. Under Kate's hand he feels drained, slack. He sits down on the bed like an old, old man. Satan pads in and noses under the bed. 'Bloody dog,' whispers Owen. There's a gulp or two. Satan comes out with a guilty look and a dusty square of bread in his mouth: he runs from the room. Kate kneels down to see. In the shadow, in the dust, are heaps of curled-up sandwiches, mounds of stale toast, a plate with what looks like ancient but untouched lasagne, plates of things not possible to be identified, some shrivelled fruit. A plate of the Mexican something from last week.

Alice struggles up and punches Owen's arms and back. 'What're you doing!' She's weeping again. 'You're skin and bone! What the hell are you doing, you're my brother, you're my friend!'

Owen doesn't shrink from the pummelling. Rather, he seems to relax into it. Alice winds her arms round him tight. 'You're a thread!' she weeps. 'You're nothing!'

He gives a weak smile. 'Not nothing enough,' he says.

Still kneeling, Kate gazes at her children. Each child she loves the best. What a dreadful, hollow feeling in her chest, what a wave of shame, up and over her whole self. Where's Richard? she thinks. Where's their father when they need his help, when I don't know how to handle things any more? It's horrifying, how negligent she's been, how heedless Richard's been. Surely, surely, Richard should have seen. She'd seen, how thin Owen was, how he picked at food . . . She gives herself a mental punch on the jaw. 'Owen, if you're not eating, what happens to the food I buy? It's not all under there. I can't keep up with all the food that disappears – '

'Oh, shit,' breathes Jessica. She and Owen share a wry movement of their eyebrows, then look at Kate. Jessica's defiant and ashamed.

'You took it to Honk,' says Kate.

Jess thrusts her hands into her armpits, hunches her shoulders. 'And some of his friends. They needed it. An' Alice, sorry 'bout your quilt.'

Alice puts her head on her knees, wraps her arms over herself. 'You didn't have to take it. All you had to do was ask. I might have given it. All you had to do was say, Jess. Bloody sister! Bloody O!'

Owen and Jess are watching, waiting for Kate to say something. She feels like the pivot of a merry-go-round with a whole new set of horses that haven't been firmly bolted on yet. The Owen horse, the Jessica and Mrs Ferlin horses, everything whirls crazily around and she can't get a good glimpse through a thickening curtain of rage.

Richard marches up the stairs that creak and tremble, and the carpet whines. 'Ah, there you are. Why aren't you at your books, Brain. I'm off to golf. Martin's booked a round at Remuera. High time I beat that bloody Daney, poor old Daney's getting past it, that's my guess.' He gives a loud laugh and then a small-f frown. 'I did tell you, didn't I.'

He didn't, but, 'Have fun,' says Kate as he ducks down the stairs again first, so won't hear the tone in which she spits, 'It's so nice that you and Martin have so much to share! *In common!*'

'What?' says Alice.

'What?' say Owen and Jessica.

'Mum?' all three say at once.

Richard is off to golf. So everyone can cry if they want to without being Frowned at. But I won't cry, thinks Kate, I won't.

They're in the sunroom. Owen's room was too smelly to stay in even when they'd cleared out under the bed. Alice and Jessica are sharing a big box of tissues, wiping their eyes. Even Owen's using it to blow his nose.

Alice punches him again. 'Quit that!' he says, which makes Kate feel momentarily more hopeful for him.

'I knew you'd think it was Owen,' says Jessica. 'But we've got so much, Mum, an' you already do such a lot for other people. And Honk an' them haven't got anything. It was only a bag or two of things each week – well, three, maybe – an' I made them promise never to come round here and – sorry!' She looks at Owen, makes as if to punch him too, but buries her head on his chest instead.

Kate holds out her arms and Jess comes into them. 'Take

something to your Honk if you want to. But tell me first, OK?'
Jess nods. 'Have you been wagging school to see your Honk?
Jessica?'

Jess snivels. 'I was nearly there all the time.'

'Did you see what Owen was doing? Did you know he
wasn't eating?' Jess buries her head more determinedly into
Kate's shoulder. That's answer enough. 'Do I need to see Mrs
Ferlin?' Jess's head rolls to and fro on Kate's shoulder in a no!
no! no!

'Don't blame Jess,' says Owen. 'Let's face it, Mum, I was
trying not to eat, that's all. I couldn't have kept it up for long.
I'm not even very good at being anorexic.' Alice hits him again
and pulls another Snowtex from the box.

'And you,' Kate says to Owen. 'What are you going to do?'
Bloody Richard, she's thinking, bloody bloody Richard! And
bloody bloody me.

'Well, could I start with breakfast?' he says, tangling a hand
in his fringe to twist it down in his old way. The girls laugh,
and gasp a little more. Jess untangles herself from Kate and hugs
Alice. There's another muffled sorry: sorry for the quilt and
pillow, sorry for Owen, sorry for everything.

'There's too much sorry, and not enough doing,' says Kate.
'You're homesick? Don't give in, do something about it. Sorry
for the street kids? What good's a can of baked beans going to
do! And sorry for yourself?' She glares at Owen. 'Don't let
things trap you, damn it!'

Get angry, shake the cage! she wants to say. Rattle the bars
until the door flies open, so you're out and flying free. She flexes
her mental wings and yes, they stretch right out. 'Awk!' says
Kate. 'I'm going to make breakfast and then I'm going to ram
it down your throats, my little loves.'

'Hang on,' says Alice. 'Mum? What did you mean? In
Owen's room. To Dad.'

'Bacon and eggs.' Kate's very brisk.

Alice pulls her back from the sunroom door. 'Mum.' Strange, how they all have a note of Richard in their voices when they're being stern. Alice gets A's for her assignments. Alice guesses, as Kate feared she might. She says. In so many words. 'He's having an affair.' Four words.

But Kate's bright too, extremely talented. She's Sarah Bernhardt, Laurence Olivier and Rin Tin Tin. 'I think he'd like to,' Kate tells her children carefully, biting each word as if it's a lump of red hot lava. 'I'm taking steps. Don't fret.'

'Have one yourself. I would!' says Jessica.

'Who with?' asks Alice. For a second Kate thinks Alice is asking who she would have an affair with. But Owen begins to suggest names. Women's names.

'Mary what's-it, that staff nurse with the bust? No, Dad couldn't be so gross. Mrs Jeffries, nah, Hamilton's too far – '

Kate blinks. They're not taking this very seriously. But then she has made them believe it's just a gleam in Richard's eye, not a reality.

'Not Greta Daney!' Alice gasps with disbelief. 'She looks like a stewardess. "Ooh Richard dear – admire me and I'll undo your tray table!" '

The young ones roll around on the floor, howling, putting on imaginary oxygen masks and going through the rescue drill.

Kate nips out to fry the bacon. With luck, they'll leave it at that.

As the bacon sizzles and begins to smell delicious and she stands there turning it with a spatula, hearing the girls still shrieking in the sunroom, Owen puts a hand on her arm. She jumps, startled.

'True though, eh?' Owen hooks up a strip of bacon and takes a bite. 'Bet I know when. Squash. It's probably Thursdays. Right?'

'You couldn't possibly know.' Kate keeps her eyes on the sizzling pan.

'Come off it, Mum. I've been around.' He puts the bacon back in the pan and licks his fingers.

Kate looks at her son. He's skinny, pale under his tan. But he isn't a child now.

chapter twenty-five

Owen still isn't eating much. But he's trying, with more than chocolate bars. Kate wanted to tell Richard, but Owen asked her not to. 'I'll do it by myself. I will go to a GP if you like. But don't tell Dad.' Kate had to agree. Not a good time to let Richard know, he's too full of himself for winning at golf with his new clubs. 'Daney was called away. Ha! Emergency delivery. I claim a moral victory!'

Richard would dismiss Owen's problem as only another silly phase, which would erode Owen's self-esteem a little more just when things might be starting to improve. If she told, it would give away Jessica's secret too. You can blame her for concealing Owen's problem, but you can't blame teenagers for being altruistic. They grow out of it given a few weeks, like pimples and puppy fat – anorexia too, she hopes. Kate's sure Jess will move from street kids, to Greenpeace, to anti-vivisection in the space of months. The less fuss made, the more quickly Jess'll get bored with each Burning Social Issue and move onto the next. It's like the hairstyles. Trying everything out. Why worry?

However. On Tuesday, while Owen is at his Helco interview, while Jessica's baking a carrot cake for Honk and making a God-awful mess in the process but she's sworn she'll clean it up, and while Alice is flying back to Christchurch, Kate tries to think things through again. Should she still worry for herself? Richard exploded on Wednesday, but he's been normal (oh

God) all weekend. The affair must be coming to a natural end. Maybe it has already.

So who will Greta think it's her right to sample next, to stop herself from being bored? Tom Lingate? Ick. Not Kate's problem.

When Richard comes home late, his sports bag full of genuinely sweat-sodden gear, she asks if he's playing again on Thursday. 'Yes,' he says.

An angry clunk of pain inside her. He moves uncomfortably when she stares at him. 'What?' says Richard.

'You're in danger of overdoing it.' In her own voice she hears the quiet note of warning. He must be really thick if he can't hear it too. So be it, thinks Kate.

She won't risk Greta and Richard arguing over the rumours Libby and she invented at lunch. A healed lovers' tiff would be a disaster. So sabotage it is, thinks Kate. Another migraine Thursday coming up.

Wednesday night. Kate has made filo pastry parcels of broccoli and cheese. Delicious. If Kate knew for certain what an orgasm was, she'd say these were as good as one. Filo is something you need time to savour. Filo, you can't rush – it would flake all over your agenda.

Owen has eaten half a filo parcel. He's drunk a glass of milk. Satan's expecting the rest of the parcel.

The Mazda MX5 comes gunning up the drive. Kate does wish Mr I'm-Entitled-to-Anything wouldn't show off like that.

With a tiny grin, Owen gets up. 'Can I have a lager, Mum?'

'You don't have to ask.' Lager has many calories.

'Have one with me,' he says to her and Jessica. He opens three bottles, hands Kate hers as Richard walks in. 'To me,' he says. 'You'll drink to this, Dad. I'm moving out. Couple of weeks yet. I'll wait till I get my first pay, if that's all right by Mum.'

Kate and Jessica cry, 'You got the job!' Satan barks. Owen smiles, wide as the harbour bridge.

'Another bloody menswear store, I suppose.' But Richard says it nicely.

'With Helco, Dad.' He raises a hand to prevent Richard's my-contacts-have-paid-off-say-thank-you-to-me smile from expanding too far. 'Mum pulled strings.' He's going to be a gofer. He'll ride his bike round town delivering, picking up. He'll get a bike allowance. He'll photocopy, collate, organise mail-outs for the Helco PR and Communications team. He'll be a dogsbody. It's a job.

'You won't get far at Helco with your seventh form maths and science.' Richard shakes Owen's hand and sits on the sofa, asking for a whisky.

Owen offers the rest of his lager. 'It's up to me, isn't it? They've got training programmes.' He fetches another bottle for himself. Owen's mouth curls up at one side. 'I'll see you're right for travel money, Dad.'

Richard is like Queen Victoria, prim-lipped for a second. But a chuckle erupts. Soon, Kate knows, he'll take Owen's joke as his: my son's got a job with Helco, I'll be off to Paris next, no worries.

Kate knows it's not fair to see the faults of those you love as she's doing now, watching Richard suffer the lager (Mr Observe-Me-As-a-Martyr) when he really wants a double Johnny Walker. You're not meant to notice the half-baked jests that grow more stale each year. Nor the skid marks on the undies and the fact that they never take the undies to the laundry by themselves, or the way they pick their noses when they think you're not looking and flick the little grey balls on the floor. If you do see, you're meant to think it's cute, adorable. If you love them. OK, thinks Kate, I've done all that for over twenty years and:

the constant drip has worn away the stone.

'Squash tomorrow, Dad?' Owen's voice is natural, curious, rimmed with a lovely glow of sarcasm. He winks at Kate as he bends to pat Satan. 'Thought I might come too.'

'Ah,' says Richard. 'Ah, already made arrangements, all under control.' But the vehicle of Richard's home-&-love life is soaring on remote, on Kate's pre-set plan. This part is called the mopping up operation. It could be termed the rinsing of the dishcloth.

Kate tells Owen she's capable of handling things herself, that he's to sort out his new flat, start packing and so on, ask at the dairy down the road if he can't find boxes in the garage.

First, she phones the school. She asks Mrs Ferlin to use the answerphone if Kate's not home and she wants to speak urgently about Jessica, and they promise to leave actual messages for each other in future, not just notes to call back.

Then Kate sets to.

This time she doesn't wear disguise. But at the same time, to heck with fashion and the way she ought to look. She puts on her set of black embroidered underwear. She paints her nails crimson. Her hands are elegant again, the bite mark's healed and her fingernails are long. She wears the bold, red gypsy dress she bought in Sydney. It floats and clings. She slips her feet into the Bellinis from the Day of the Invoice. She puts heavy gold hoops in her ears and dabs Poison down her cleavage. Her hair is an untamed mane, like a movie star's.

'Come on, Satan!' calls Kate. He hops into the back of the Chariot. With her, she has a bottle of water and his untippable dish. Two o'clock. She has an appointment in Parnell just after three. Before she leaves, she calls the Daneys' number: their answerphone is on. She doesn't leave a message. She drives to outer Remmers.

The Mazda isn't where it was last time but doesn't take long to find. She stops the Chariot nearby. She drives Satan and the MX5 a few doors down from Greta's. She and Satan walk back to the Chariot, she takes it to the Daneys' too and parks outside. There's still a trace of compost on the drive, though no sign of little Cuddles. Kate doubts that Richard and Greta are having a very cuddly time today, not after the seeds she and Libby planted over lunch. I'll give you 'pleasure at home', she thinks. She winds the car windows down to let air circulate, puts Satan's dish on the floor and pours water into it. 'You won't have long to wait, my hero,' she reassures him.

She walks back to the Mazda, swinging the car keys, humming. It's a new song she's making up about an oleander bush, so poisonous and so beautiful.

In the Remuera shopping centre Kate wanders through an arcade till half an hour is up, and finds a phone. She calls the Daneys' number. Martin's voice speaks the answerphone message: *Gidday! We're busy right now . . .*

Aren't you, though, thinks Kate. 'It's Kate,' she says. 'Kate Wildburn. It's some time after 2.30 on Thursday afternoon. I hope you've got the sound turned up on this. Greta, I have a message for Richard. I can't look after Satan this afternoon. He's Richard's dog, after all. I'm going into town, and I'm taking the smaller car.' If Satan's alone in a car for more than half an hour, he has a particularly tortured howl. Kate feels a swell of love for him.

She drives now to Perky Lorrence's place, next door to his sister's where Libby hung cherubs in the living room. They talk business, sitting on a red leather sofa. A bear rug with huge fangs and a wrinkled snout lies doggo on the floor. Kate thinks it would be even more frightening than Perky if you met it in an empty warehouse.

Kate still thinks he's mad and says so. But Perky growls that he goes by his nose (the spotty apple one) and it says gamble on her. 'Libby will keep you in line. That woman!' He chuckles.

'Kept that sister of mine in line and that's something I could never do. Women. Can't understand 'em. That's the delight of them, I'd say. Never pays to understand a woman.' He's had a contract drawn up. Libby has already signed. Kate reads it through, still teetering; should she be trusted?

Perky sighs, a sort of grumbling in his bronchial tubes. She glances up. He's gazing at her dress. 'Ah. A woman looking like a woman.' Perky Lorrence sighs again in his spotty apple voice.

Kate returns to the contract. It would be such a poke in the eye for Richard if she . . . God. Richard doesn't carry the Chariot's keys with him. She's definitely gone too far this time. With a deep, excited breath she signs her name.

'What's life without a risk?' rumbles Perky when he sees her back to the car.

The Mazda whizzes up St Stephens Avenue and into Parnell Road. It's actually lots of fun to gun this thing.

Helco Tower's on the corner coming up. Kate's happy: everything's gone just to plan. She sees an empty parking place. Pop up and say thank you. No harm in that. Good PR, even, for Richard's sake – it would be the last twist of the knife to do something positive for Richard today. Marketing, 7th Floor. John might be in a meeting. He might be out of town. It doesn't matter. Even if she has to leave a message, she will have said thanks nicely.

His receptionist speaks into an intercom, and John's voice speaks back. Surprised. Pleased? Slightly flustered?

He opens the door of his office. He does seem surprised, but pleased as well. His moustache gives a whiffle. He waves her through, pushes the door shut behind her.

It's a very impressive office: he must be solid. She'd absolutely trust him to fly her in the outback. There's a very wide desk. There's thick carpet and on the wall a reproduction

Don Binney bird, pompous and ominous in a bland blue sky.

'That'd make a nice roast,' says Kate. 'It would serve it right.'

John gives a bark of laughter. He's stopped looking surprised and now looks energetic, as if he doesn't know what might happen but he'll enjoy, and manage, whatever it is. Through the windows, there's a view of the harbour, Rangitoto lying on the water like a perfect shape drawn by a liberated mathematician. Shapes and maths. Chaos Theory. Patterns. Kate doesn't understand Chaos Theory yet, but something about it appeals to her. She'll visit Unity Books in High Street and buy something on it; all the trendies buy their books at Unity and she did say she was going into town.

'I don't want to hold you up,' says Kate. He whiffles his moustache again and gestures to an armchair.

'Coffee?' asks John. 'Something stronger? You've something to celebrate, about Owen.' He opens a small oak cabinet and it's a fridge, well stocked. Kate feels so happy: this is all completely legitimate, but exhilarating, like in the movies when people visit other people in big expensive offices and all sorts of subterfuge is going on, unspoken. 'Gin? I'll make you a Manhattan.' There are cherries and olives, and a lemon ready-sliced. It's the big picture, in that little fridge.

'No, honestly,' says Kate. 'Well, yes. I'd love one.'

But he sits on the armchair's arm. 'They found the platypus in 1790-odd. Scientists, I mean. I'm sure the Aborigines had known since the Dreamtime. They thought it was a hoax. Tried to take its beak off with a pair of scissors.'

'It used to be called the duckmole,' says Kate. 'I wanted to thank you straight away. About Owen.' She holds out her hand for shaking. Still sitting, he takes it. His rough-backed, warm-palmed hand. It's all right to kiss him, she thinks without thinking – it's not her mind that's thinking, but something deeper, like Chaos. Just to say thank you, urges Chaos. So,

'Thank you,' she says. And a peck, bird-light, on the cheek near his moustache.

There's a short moment which seems to shimmer at the edges. John looks as if there's been a little earthquake. 'My pleasure. I'll get you that Manhattan.' He stands. He's just as tall as she is. The shimmering's still there. He pecks her too. On the mouth. Bird-light.

She's stunned. It's true. Some kisses are electric. They look at each other as if something completely awful has just happened.

Something completely amazing. Amazing and scandalous.

And awful. But mostly, it's amazing.

And . . .

chapter twenty-six

K ate arrives home just on five, with her book on Chaos from Unity (that's nice, she thinks, Unity and Chaos) and a light heart (light but brimful of unity and chaos). She's incredibly happy. This afternoon she saw Morality, like a little gnome, sit on a metaphorical window ledge on a 7th Floor, tip his hat and slide out of her life holding an umbrella not a parachute. She is free: to decide whatever she wants. She hopes Richard will be annoyed that she's signed the contract with Perky. And she hopes he's sorted out the car keys. But, she thinks, I'm too unified by chaos to be particularly bothered what he thinks, about Perky or the Chariot.

Owen's in his room packing books, CDs and running shoes into cardboard boxes. 'Hey, what's with Dad!' he calls when Kate comes up to change out of the gypsy dress into something more suitable for cooking a quick stroganoff.

Richard has been home in a taxi, roared around yelling for the spare keys, took ages to find them, kept roaring, and disappeared in the taxi again.

'Interesting message on the answerphone, too,' says Owen. 'When I came back from the dairy – I went to get the cartons.'

'Yes?' says Kate.

'Mrs Daney. She said, "Kate! All right!" That's all she said.' Owen gives his lop-sided grin. 'Not what you'd call specific or articulate. But I guess you did it, Mum. She said, "All right. All right! *All right!*" I haven't erased it. Thought you'd like to hear it for yourself.'

Kate smiles. She's pleased of course, but doesn't really care any more. Not since the gnome slipped out the window.

'Amelia phoned, too. Couple of minutes ago.' Owen's head is in the wardrobe. He flings a pair of gumboots out: why would he have gumboots in his wardrobe? Being a normal young person, Kate supposes thankfully. 'She sounded pretty hyper. That's usual, I guess, for Amelia.'

In the main bedroom, Kate dials her sister. Amelia's more than hyper. She's hysterical.

'Drystan – he's come back – he's hanging round outside! Kate, I can't get rid of him and Barry's due home soon!'

The Warrior Queen's stomach gives a cramp. Her period's started – a few days late, but the agitation of today has helped at last – so she takes care of that with feminum perteck-shum before she runs out to the Mazda. As she backs down the drive, the Chariot arrives. Richard stops behind her so she can't get past.

'What in hell do you mean by it!' He jumps out, neck and shoulders swollen like a bullfrog's. 'What do you mean em-barrassing me like that!'

With a whine of anguish Satan shoves out of the car where he's been cooped up since two o'clock, and cocks his leg on a dahlia. Kate hops out of the Mazda, into the Chariot. She ignores Richard: he can send her a memo if he likes, he can set up a meeting. Satan stops mid-pee and leaps to join her with another whine of pain as he bumps his sore leg. Richard's voice is high with panic, 'What? Where are you – Kate!' She slams the door. The gypsy dress is caught but she takes off out of the driveway, over to Amelia's lickety-split. *Parp! parp!* goes Little Noddy's horn. The 5.30 traffic's hell.

The turquoise Datsun's parked inside Amelia's drive, half on the grass. Amelia might at least find a lover who can drive adequately, thinks Kate. Gorgeous, breakfast-haired Drystan is banging on the front door. Satan bounces up and down inside the car: he hasn't seen Amelia for weeks.

There she is in the window, flapping her hands. Satan whines with excitement: she isn't usually so pleased to see him. In fact, she's never been pleased to see him before. Kate can tell, by the way he begins to smell, that he's the most excited he's ever been in his ten-year-old life. 'Mind your leg, it isn't healed yet,' she warns as she lets him out.

Amelia opens the window. 'Go get him, Satan!' She points at Drystan. 'Run him off!'

Satan is Lassie. He's the Big Bad Wolf and the Avatar of He Who Protects All Women. Drystan backs away, stammering. Satan stalks closer. He doesn't snarl. He simply stares and dribbles. Drystan makes a dash for the Datsun and clambers in. Satan dances round; it's incredible how balletic he is now he's forgotten his bandage. It's incredible how he hangs in the air like a big brown comma, how he prances and threatens. How he won't be called off when Drystan starts the engine, swerves across the grass. How he gets in the way when Drystan bumps into Barry's old V8. How he is hurled against the concrete gate post, and how he lies there like a brown full stop.

Something's happened to Kate's chest. She feels hot and frozen, all at the same time. Satan. She steps closer. Satan?

Amelia comes out followed by Rebecca. They stand beside Kate, looking down. At Satan.

'What did that man want?' Rebecca's shrill with distress. 'Who was he, Mum? Aunt Kate?'

'He thought your Mum was very sexy, 'Becca.' Kate hears the breath fill up in her sister's lungs. She wonders if she'll ever get breath back properly into her own. 'And you can't blame him for that. But you can blame him for not taking no for an answer.'

'Heavy duty!' Rebecca stares at her mother with a touch

of awe, then back at Satan. 'Can he go to prison for killing a dog?'

But maybe Satan isn't dead. Kate doesn't want him to be dead. She won't leave him. She won't go inside, just in case he snorts and wags his head and staggers to his feet. Kate snorts, she wags her head, she staggers to show him how to do it.

'Oh, hon.' Amelia takes Kate's arm, but she shakes her sister off. She practises breathing. Amelia tells Rebecca to fetch the cask of Blenheimer Dry, and persuades Kate to move across the grass. They sit on the front steps, watching the big brown crumpled thing. Amelia pours wine for them both and they practise breathing and drinking, and they're very drunk and both crying, tears leaking out as if they've been punctured, and so is 'Becca crying and drinking a Coke, and it starts to get cold so Amelia wraps them all in a quilted rug from Trade Aid, and Barry the Brave comes home.

Dear brave Barry doesn't ask any questions. With a kind look on his dear round face, he just digs a hole in the back yard.

It has to be a very big hole. As big as Barry. Kate estimates it would hold over forty possums. Barry's being very good about it, really. Satan has saved the V8 from worse damage.

chapter twenty-seven

Kate gets up on Friday and wears the black dress she bought in Sydney. She plays the 'Oleander Song' all day. She plays it most of Saturday too. She doesn't talk. She plays the song for Satan. His oleander, where he won't sleep any more. It's a song to a hero. Satan the Defender.

It was going to be a song about poisoning Richard. It was pretty clear that Richard was about to have plans for taking Satan to the vet. He might even have brought a lethal injection home himself.

No, Kate doesn't really believe that. It would be illegal. She believes Richard may have wanted to, mind you. He may have coveted an illegal lethal injection. Some things, it's wrong to covet.

Richard is a sinner, thinks Kate. He broke two Commandments. He committed adultery and coveted his neighbour's wife. Not that the Daneys live close by, but Kate doesn't think that's material.

Kate isn't a sinner. She does covet someone's ex-husband, but she's looked up Exodus and it only mentions coveting wives and houses, manservants and maidservants, oxen and asses. So neighbours are only men, according to the Bible and it's not a sin to covet a neighbour, just what belongs to one. Good on the Bible, thinks Kate. And she hasn't committed adultery. Not yet. Oh, yes though, she is a sinner because she takes the name of the Lord in vain. Not that she gives a stuff about that. But it means:

the world is full of sinners

as she puts it, in silent words, in a new verse of the 'Oleander Song'.

Richard edges into the living room. Saturday night. Owen and Jess, red-eyed, have spent all day in their rooms or on the phone to their friends to get comforted, especially Owen from his apparently new girlfriend. Red-eyed, like Kate.

It's no life without Satan.

Kate adds it to the song.

'You've played that thing to death.' Richard, hands awkward by his sides. 'You haven't even cooked. We have to talk.'

Kate swivels round on the piano stool. 'Everything's all right, isn't it?'

Richard's hands dangle even more awkwardly. The Barometer's a funny shade of pink.

Kate shakes her head. 'Well, of course it's not. Satan's dead. Mind you, now you mention it, we haven't talked about it for a while. What's first with you these days? Work still? Or me?' She speaks pleasantly, lightly. Kate has to be her own Defender now. But she's made it easy for Richard. When the kids were little, if she gave them a choice she always put the thing she wanted them to choose last. Always worked. It was easier for them to remember the last thing so they'd choose it. She's interested to see if it will work with Richard. But probably not. He's been on a special kind of ladder – one rung means he's entitled to anything anyone else has, the next rung means his self image depends on what other people think of him, and the next means he's Mr Hard-Done-By so the next rung means he can't admit to having an affair. Before you know, the ladder's twisted into one of those horrible wheels that mice use, round and round and round.

His eyes are full of disbelief. His mouth opens and shuts. 'But you – when you – what about – ' He must realise that he's come close to admitting adultery out loud. 'I'll get another dog,' he says.

'I'm tired of looking after your dogs,' Kate replies. 'If we get another dog I'd like it to be mine. Richard? What comes first?'

His mouth opens and closes again. 'It's obvious. Work has to come first. If it wasn't for my work.' He speaks as if the words taste slightly off. 'Without that, we'd all be nowhere.'

'Just so I know,' she says. And she does know – he has to say work comes first, otherwise he'd be admitting she's won. Just as she doesn't want a divorce because that would be admitting that she's lost. Oh yes, she's lost. She's won, and lost, and it's hard to find her breath, just like when she saw Satan lying so still. But she smiles a romantic novel smile, looking up at her husband's confused-but-turning-to-relief eyes and mouth. She doesn't think romantic heroines ever have periods, though; it's time she had another Ponstan.

She turns back to the upright and plays the song again to annoy Richard. It's very sad, the song, and also what Richard has just said. Because Kate knows it oughtn't to be true. 'I've said yes to Perky Lorrence,' she says above the arpeggios that are Satan dancing and the sombre bass notes that are Barry digging the hole.

'Well!' Richard sounds as if he's braced himself. A so-we're-back-to-normal kind of brace. 'I'll have to meet him. He might be good for a bit of sponsorship. He's got some public spirit. Yes.'

Kate throws in another set of arpeggios – Satan ascending into heaven: the song gets longer every time. 'I don't think so. Ten years ago, he gave a private hospital three feet of his upper colon. He reckons that's enough for anyone to give to medicine.' She strokes a set of chords out of the ivory keys: the Gates of Heaven opening. 'By the way, the Visa statement came today.'

She's seen him looking at it. The large amount from Fleurs d'Amour. The bill from Stirling Sports. The amount from Private Dick: it wouldn't take much intelligence to work out what Security & Investigations Inc. (Licensed) means. Richard made the statement jerk and flutter when he saw the list of agricultural supply centres on it too.

'Are you . . . ' Richard rests a hand, heavy but tentative, on her shoulder. She stops playing. 'We're all right, aren't we, Kate?'

A quiet trill on the keys: Satan having a quick pee on the gate post before running in to romp unbandaged with the seraphim, and he's sure to wriggle under the fence to play next door in Valhalla.

'Excuse me a minute.'

Richard follows her to the bedroom. 'Kate. Aren't we, Kate? What's that?' he asks as she presses a blue and yellow capsule from the wrapping and puts it in her mouth.

She shows him the packet and its picture of the emblematic woman with the disconnected head.

'Who prescribed this? Did you see Martin? I was going to speak to Martin about that.'

She shakes her head. 'Over the counter. My counsellor told me.'

Richard's mouth drops open for the third time. 'Your what!'

Kate shrugs. 'Not anyone you know, don't worry. I was upset for a while so I saw a counsellor. But there's not much profit in that.' Her tone says, *because I don't really care.*

Richard's shoulders seem to shrink. That, she sees, is the worst thing she could have let him know. That she doesn't really care. But no one has admitted anything out loud. So after a moment or two he puts a hand around her waist and *one two three* into his chassez reverse turn, and she moves out of his arms to clap silently to the silent orchestra, and Richard bows to her.

And as he straightens up his shoulders can – and do – become torpedo-like, and The Barometer can – and does – return to pinkish brown, and he can walk out of the bedroom and down the stairs and into his study where he'll probably turn on his 14-inch Sanyo, put a fresh sheet of paper on his desk and head it: MEETINGS FOR MAY & JUNE.

She does care, of course. How unfortunate, thinks Kate, that telling lies is an important part of learning to be adult. How very heavy duty.

chapter twenty-eight

K ate has learned to justify anything. She's learned how anger can carry you along and help you justify growing out of your ambition to be the only faithful wife in the twentieth century.

It's like being altruistic or homesick – you get past it once you've rattled the bars enough and got your head through, and a wing, and a scaly little foot with talons on, and whee! out flicks the other wing.

She can justify lusting after John Colin – how strange it feels, but at least it's feeling something besides stunned, enraged and empty. If she has an affair with him, she may be helping Richard. If she decides to consider it that way. Because Helco may look more favourably on helping the gastro clinical project.

So if she sleeps with John (misleading expression), isn't it saving Richard from a fate which, to him, would be worse than death? Staying on the ignominious lower rungs of the surgical ladder of in-house social standing?

It would make her:

```
       the most useful wife
    of the nineteen-nineties.
```

That sounds excruciatingly boring. But. After all. She could use it, to justify the affair if Richard ever found out.

After all:

```
Growing up is learning how to be a useful
member of whatever society fate has made you
                    part of.
```

That sounds boring too. But Richard would have to agree with it. There's justification for you, thinks Kate.

And what she's really decided is that she doesn't have to justify a thing. All she has to do is enjoy it. She doesn't want her story to have a moral – how could it? The gnome called Morality opened his umbrella and jumped out the window.

So she doesn't have to justify such lust. In her. In herself, who always thought these feelings only came between the covers of novels, in films, imagination, fantasy.

She knows now. She was right. The main reason for having an affair is:

the he of it, the she of it, the fantasy come true.

The sound of his voice on the phone makes her feel a jewel, flower, unmistakably woman.

'I'm taking the day off work,' he says. 'Have lunch with me?'

A whole day? Off work? For her? And he sounds uncertain, as if he's worried she might say no, as if he badly wants this. Her. For a whole day. That's hours.

He could lose his job, if this were ever known. He'd take such risks. For her, the she of it. Or for the risk, the risk of it.

A whole day of risk! Heavy duty.

Even thinking about John wakes up parts of her body that must have been sleeping forever. He'd take time for this. So this is part of what Amelia means. Before the bungy jump.

Kate has never known that women's loins can feel so

passionate, so stirred just from thinking about someone. She hasn't known that her lungs can take in so much air, be so alive. She didn't know the skin on her arms, shoulders, belly, thighs would yearn and long and tingle just because –

Amelia should have told her years ago. Oh that's not fair, thinks Kate, she tried but the truth is, Amelia doesn't really know. Not about the he of it. The she.

It would be driving – (over the bridge but not to see Lyllian Spicer) – it would be walking – (up the path to John's townhouse in Devonport) – in a personal electrical storm.

Lightning flashes through her breasts. She's saturated in a downpour of desire.

She'd walk into his living room. A coffee table, with a bottle of Zinfandel, a wedge of brie, crusty French bread on a lacquer tray, black olives in a china dish, sliced melon. And – a pomegranate?

His sandy hair, large hands, the humorous moustache.

'I thought there ought to be a pomegranate.' His hands out, palms up, waiting. Would that decide it? Even though by then, the bedroom visible through an open door? She could still say no (though having got that far, it would be an awful let-down if she did).

But. A pomegranate. The colour of a parrot's eyes, orange, black, and wicked. Golden. Ebony. Sun and night.

The fantasy. The he of it, the she. For a man who offered pomegranates, she could vow to be:

*☞ the most accommodating mistress
in the history of the world! ☞*

And, lying on his bed. The floor strewn with black embroidered underwear, a Hane's T-shirt and a pair of Y-fronts.

Together, they are appetite, completion. She is a crystal glass, an amphitheatre, white-hot, shaped into a bowl to hold him. He is cognac, swirling amber. She is light, transparent, drenched with him.

They are subversion, secrets, they're the possibilities of scandal, shock and horror. Guerrilla fighters plunging through the jungle of desire. And Kate not bothered by his bits at all.

So this is what it's all about, thinks Kate. No wonder people lie for it and cheat and steal and die for it. It is all true. All. True.

The Warrior Queen is laid to rest — sweet dreams.

Or – just reality?